Mount Everest

Namche Bazaar

A FREDDIE MALONE ADVENTURE

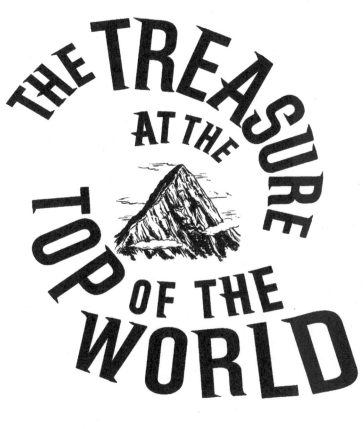

THE TREASURE AT THE TOP OF THE WORLD

CLIVE MANTLE

AWARD PUBLICATIONS LIMITED

ISBN 978-1-78270-321-1

Text copyright © 2018 Clive Mantle
Cover design by Patrick Knowles
Photograph of Everest by Daniel Prudek/Shutterstock.com
Photograph of Namche Bazaar by Raisa Suprun/Shutterstock.com
Map and text illustration by Angie Hewitt
This edition copyright © Award Publications Limited

First published by Award Publications Limited 2018

Published by Award Publications Limited,
The Old Riding School, Welbeck,
Worksop, S80 3LR

www.awardpublications.co.uk

18 1

Printed in the United Kingdom

For Harry

If–

If you can keep your head when all about you
    Are losing theirs and blaming it on you,
If you can trust yourself when all men doubt you,
    But make allowance for their doubting too;
If you can wait and not be tired by waiting,
    Or being lied about, don't deal in lies,
Or being hated, don't give way to hating,
    And yet don't look too good, nor talk too wise:

If you can dream – and not make dreams your master;
    If you can think – and not make thoughts your aim;
If you can meet with Triumph and Disaster
    And treat those two imposters just the same;
If you can bear to hear the truth you've spoken
    Twisted by knaves to make a trap for fools,
Or watch the things you gave your life to, broken,
    And stop and build 'em up with worn-out tools:

If you can make one heap of all your winnings
    And risk it on one turn of pitch-and-toss,
And lose, and start again at your beginnings
    And never breathe a word about your loss;
If you can force your heart and nerve and sinew
    To serve your turn long after they are gone,
And so hold on when there is nothing in you
    Except the will which says to them: "Hold on!"

If you can talk with crowds and keep your virtue,
    Or walk with Kings – nor lose the common touch,
If neither foes nor loving friends can hurt you,
    If all men count with you, but none too much;
If you can fill the unforgiving minute
    With sixty seconds' worth of distance run,
Yours is the Earth and everything that's in it,
    And—which is more—you'll be a Man, my son!

Rudyard Kipling, 1895

The Treasure at the Top of the World

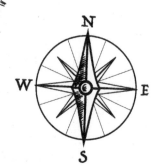

Everest Base Camp

Gorak Shep

Dughla

Pheriche • • Dingboche

Pangboche

Thyangboche

• Namche Bazaar

NEPAL

• Luckla

Mount Everest

N

W   E

S

Prologue

In a very beautiful and sacred place, an extremely long way from where you are reading these words, stood a huge wooden statue of a happy, smiling God. He guarded some priceless treasures, which any man would marvel at and a terrible few would seek to possess.

And, in a very dark and squalid place, which is also an extremely long way from you, and even further away from the huge statue of the smiling God, there sat three ruthless and villainous men, huddled together in a grimy basement.

These shadowy figures sat hunched over a small table under a single shaft of light, studying an ornate and ancient map. The beam picked out its amazing intricacies, as well as the rising smoke from a pungent and highly distinctive cigar that the largest of the three men smoked as if his life depended on it. He and his fair-haired companion listened with grim determination as the oldest man of the trio told them excitedly of his wicked plan.

It was really a very simple scheme: to steal the priceless relics from under the nose of the mighty statue, so that they would sit forever in the old man's collection, for his eyes and his enjoyment only. The man was impossibly rich and very used to the two men opposite acquiring the objects of his desire. Indeed, some years before, they had stolen the very map laid out before them from an ancient order of Celtic wizards, who had been searching for it high and low ever since.

In truth, this latest undertaking was simple, the only difficulty being that of endurance, because the treasures were housed on a plateau set amongst the most colossal mountains on earth. But the two younger villains were well used to strenuous challenges in the execution of the old man's fiendish dreams.

His gnarled hands slid two things across the exquisitely decorated map, as if making a move on an elaborate board game, travelling from one continent to another. The first was a bulging rag doll made of red and green patchwork pieces, which contained in its hollowed stomach their expenses of $30,000. The second article was an enormous box of cigars – a present for the larger man and his personal favourites. His face lit up with a greedy smile when he saw the gift, as his sinister fair -haired companion carefully counted the money and the old collector watched them both like a hawk.

Finally, they all nodded in agreement and the old man carefully rolled up the beautiful map. All three retreated from the table like a receding fog, leaving only the solitary light to pick up the remnants of the disturbed cigar smoke as it rose into the darkness, filling the dingy *basement with its distinctive aroma. An aroma that would be impossible for anyone to forget. An aroma that would linger for an eternity, long after both the cigar and its smoker were gone.*

Chapter One

Connor knocked on the door of number 10, Normandy Avenue. It was the first gloriously hot sunny Sunday of the summer holidays. Connor had been looking forward to his best friend Freddie's birthday bash all week; to a house full of fun and laughter and most importantly, fabulous food.

The August sunshine blazed on his back as he heard footsteps from within. Freddie flung the door open wide, smiled and then winked.

"Perfect timing as usual, mate. Mum's just putting the grub out."

Freddie's real birthday wasn't until Friday, but Mrs Malone had decided that a weekend party would mean more people could attend, and she was right; the lounge, kitchen and small garden were jam-packed, resounding with the animated Irish voices of all Freddie's relatives, mixed with music and bursts of laughter.

Connor smiled at Mrs M, who was organising the table at the far end of the lounge. It was absolutely groaning with awesome food, with more large platters on every other available surface.

"Help yerself, Connor, darlin'," she said. "Thanks so much for coming. Let's look at yer, don't yer scrub up well?"

Connor mumbled his thanks and filled his plate, mainly with pork pie and salami at this first visit to the feast. He moved into the garden and spotted both of Freddie's gorgeous grown up sisters. They were helping Mr Malone, who was dashing about, servicing the glasses of his guests, looking as wiry and vibrant as usual.

Freddie was slim like his dad with a tonne of mousey brown hair. He and Connor were complete physical opposites, different in practically every way, but they were nevertheless inseparable best friends.

Ten minutes later, as Connor next refreshed his plate, the front door suddenly seemed to burst open and with his usual whirlwind entrance, Freddie's mad Uncle Patrick arrived in the centre of the lounge, wearing the loudest Hawaiian shirt ever created. He had a box of his favourite Irish beer under one arm and tucked under his other was an intriguing four-foot tube.

Freddie tugged at the strange cylinder. "What's this?"

Patrick swatted his hand away. "Ah, get arf, lad! All in good time. Patience is a virtue, and we need all the virtue we can get in this family," he said with a laugh and a glint in his dancing blue eyes.

He put down the box of beer, ruffled Connor's super-neat black hair and pointed through the doorway, saying, "Connor, I need the biggest glass you can find in that there kitchen."

With a big smile on his face and a couple of sausage rolls for the journey, Connor headed off. It wasn't a party until Uncle Patrick showed up, but it took him five minutes to get his hair back the way he wanted it.

With his best friend in great demand with all of his relatives, Connor was happy to wander about and chat to everyone. He felt like a celebrity. They all knew who he was and said things like, "So you're Freddie's famous best friend are you?" The only chat he didn't enjoy was with a really old deaf guy, a great Uncle of Freddie's, called Finnegan. However loud Connor tried to answer his questions, he couldn't make himself heard or understood. Eventually he gave up and headed off back to the buffet. As he walked away, he heard Finnegan proclaim to his equally old and deaf wife, "He's no stranger to a pork pie, is he, Kathleen!"

Connor restored his shaken confidence with a second slice of Mrs M's lemon drizzle cake.

It was soon time for Freddie to open his presents. There were console games, some cool trainers, the odd five and ten pound note and, from Kathleen and Finnegan, new school socks ("Great! Just what I need!" Freddie politely gushed). Connor watched as Freddie continued to unwrap a succession of gifts any thirteen-year-old boy would be thrilled with.

Then Uncle Patrick finally stepped forward. With outstretched arms and a mock curtsie he ceremoniously handed Freddie the mysterious cardboard tube, which he had not put down since his arrival. Connor knew that whatever was inside must be truly special. Freddie took delivery of the gift with two careful hands. He cautiously opened one end and gently shook the contents out of the tube.

There were excited gasps when an ancient-looking scroll was revealed from its depths. Connor had never seen anything like it in real life.

"Wow!" he gasped and stepped forward to help Freddie unroll the intriguing present. As they moved apart slowly, a huge antique world Map of the World was revealed between the two boys, with all the countries in different, bright colours and all the cities, deserts and mountains clearly marked. It had beautifully painted animals scattered around their home continents, and famous buildings and landmarks illustrated next to each major city. It shimmered and glowed in the August sunshine, with little sparks of light flashing from the paint pigment as the sun's rays caught it at different angles. Connor saw Patrick and Finnegan share a little smile across the hushed garden.

Freddie was speechless. It was an amazing present. He felt like it should be on display in a world famous museum, not due to be hung in the third bedroom of a suburban semi-detached house. He hugged his favourite uncle and eventually stammered, "It's the best … Thank you. It's just brilliant."

The map smelt truly wonderful; a little musty, but more like a mysterious blend of exotic spices, as if bought from a faraway street market. It radiated a sense of power. As Freddie held it, he felt a deep calm and tranquility flood through his limbs. That feeling couldn't have come at a better time, as it was an old family tradition for the Malones to perform on their birthdays and Freddie's task had been set months before. Now his big moment had arrived and a slightly wobbly Uncle Patrick tapped his near empty beer glass until silence fell amongst the expectant crowd.

"As you all know, this young man has reached

an important milestone. And in the tradition of the Malones, he will perform, perhaps the most special task of his young life, because the poem he must recite is one of the most important things ever written. It contains the wisdom of a man called Kipling – that's the poet, Connor, not the cake maker!" Connor happily blushed amongst the good-natured laughter, thrilled to be included in the speech in whatever capacity. Patrick slapped him hard on the back, reruffled his now neat again hair and continued, "Rudyard Kipling crafted a great gift for the world. A poem called 'If—'. I hereby declare that my favourite nephew—"

"You've only got one!" pitched in Mr M, as if in a double act with Patrick.

"That's as maybe, Declan, but nevertheless I still declare that if you follow the poem's wonderful advice, and strictly navigate the road ahead with your new map, there will not be a problem in life that can't be solved. May it guide you safely through all your own magnificent adventures." *It was typical Uncle Patrick*, thought Freddie. *Always slightly over-doing the build up.*

But now it was his turn. Freddie was gently thrust forward by his dad as Connor held the map and nodded encouragement. Freddie took a deep breath and began his recital. After the first line, he felt his nerves melt away and he made a sound job of reciting the poem. A huge cheer erupted at the conclusion and Freddie's mum had to be given a hankie by Kathleen, who grumbled loudly to Finnegan that she hadn't heard a single word. But Finnegan just smiled serenely as if he'd heard everything perfectly. Patrick beamed and wrapped Freddie in a giant bearhug.

Connor thought the poem and Freddie's performance were totally brilliant. During the last few climactic lines, he scanned the smiling faces and felt a rush of happiness that he was involved in the warm and happy gathering. Everyone wanted him there, especially his cool best friend – and it was all just about to get better; Freddie's birthday cake was being cut and Connor had his eye on a large side bit, which consequently had double the icing.

Chapter Two

"Sorry!" Connor heard himself saying again, as he duelled with an elderly man in a mobility buggy for pavement space by the Post Office. It wasn't that far to Freddie's house, but Connor had been in a hurry ever since Freddie's frantic 8 a.m. text. Now his phone was beeping at him again.

Are you coming?! F.

Something was definitely up. Connor sent a hasty reply, only just avoiding a reversing delivery van. That quick side-stepping thing everyone else seemed to manage so easily just wasn't part of his repertoire.

On my way. C.

They hadn't seen each other since the brilliant party. Connor had been packed off by his parents to his Auntie Cheryl's for four days of constant television, awkward conversation, and flapjack. He was desperate to catch up on all the party gossip, to discuss whether grown men should be allowed out in shirts like the one Uncle Patrick had worn, and most importantly, to see the awesome Map of the World close up.

Connor smiled at the memory of the fun afternoon, but his happy thoughts vanished as he saw a familiar gang of boys emerge from the passage by the church. He froze as the tallest of them kicked an empty can high into the air. It was Jasper and his mates, Maz, Rowan and Paul.

Connor shrunk back into a shop doorway as his heart began to beat faster. Just one laserbeam stare from Jasper's scary blue eyes was enough to make anyone shudder. Being best friends with someone as awesome as Freddie did have its downside. Jasper didn't like competition. It wasn't a great idea to be popular with teachers, classmates and girls if Jasper was around. Especially girls. Even girls from the year above, like Carrie Peterson, who once said she thought Freddie was 'cool'. Nothing could top that.

Connor had extra reason to be cautious. On the way home from school a few weeks ago, Connor and Freddie had been ambushed by Jasper and his crew outside the bakery. It had been more pushing than punching, but as they retreated Connor had tripped over Freddie and landed heavily on the pavement, miraculously leaving the chicken and mushroom slice he was holding completely intact. It could have been a lot worse had they not been saved by Chloe and Phoebe, a couple of girls from their class, who filmed the whole incident on a phone and then told Mr Coles, the Head of Year, the next day. Mr Coles had hit Jasper where it hurt most – by banning him from sports for the rest of the summer term.

So Freddie and Connor had been on red alert all summer, waiting for reprisals. Now that it was hot and sunny and everyone was out and about all day, it was only a matter of time. Connor breathed a sigh of relief as he saw them swagger noisily into the new shopping centre, shouting and smacking each other round the head. He continued on to Freddie's house the long way round, just in case.

Hurry up! F.

Five minutes later Connor stood breathless and red cheeked, pressing the Malone's front door bell. When no one answered, he headed down the side alley. He watched through the kitchen window as Mrs Malone frantically swept her loose change and car keys into her handbag. She got a shock when she looked up and then hastily unlocked the back door.

"Connor! You'll be the death of me one day, love."

"Sorry, Mrs M."

"That's OK – Listen, darlin' ... Freddie's not feeling well. Holiday Club's out, I'm afraid. I think he's got a cold coming." She flicked her long dark hair out of her way and continued to bustle around the kitchen. "There's some nasty wee marks on his face as well. Away up and see him, sweetheart." She gestured to the hall, whilst peering into a tiny mirror and hurriedly applying some mascara.

Connor headed for the stairs, by far his favourite part of Freddie's house, where the walls were crammed with photos of holidays and special occasions. There were collages of cup-final and theatre tickets and smaller cut-up photos of friends and family and Christmases and picnics, crazily overlapping with postcards and restaurant menus. Connor always saw something new.

He reached his favourite photo; Freddie's beautiful sisters at a wedding in Dublin. Totally amazing. Mollie, the eldest, lived in Cornwall and was about to have a baby, and nineteen-year-old Maddie had just left home and was a chef in a posh London restaurant. Connor tore himself away and stuck his head round Freddie's bedroom door.

"Happy birthday to you, hap— You alright?"

Connor stared at his best friend in shock. Freddie looked totally awful. There were indeed a dozen or so 'nasty wee marks' on his face, like little blisters, and he was definitely not his usual smiling self. His typically lively brown eyes looked empty. He was covered in blankets and a duvet, and yet he still seemed to be freezing.

"Does your mum know how bad you are?"

"Y–Y–Yes. I'm going to – the d–doctor if I'm no better b–by the time she g–gets back from work," Freddie stuttered.

Mrs Malone swept in and felt her son's forehead. She tutted ominously.

"Would you be an angel and keep him company today? Mrs Jackson's next door if you need her, for emergencies. And, Connor, darlin', could you heat him up some soup for lunch? There's a love. Oh! And ring me if he gets any worse." She hugged Freddie, who winced with pain.

"Sure," Connor said. He followed downstairs in her slipstream and waited while Mrs M jotted her office number on a pad.

Then she paused and said quietly, "Poor Freddie. What a way to spend his birthday. Now, you're sure you can manage?"

Connor wasn't absolutely sure, but he seemed to convince her that he could be left in charge. Mrs M opened the fridge and pushed aside an old-fashioned tin box to show him where the soup was. Connor eyed the strange tin and assumed that it must contain her sandwiches, though even he didn't fancy eating anything out of it.

Mrs M was already heading for the hall. She showed him how to lock the doors in case they went out anywhere. Connor was only half listening, because he thought it was unlikely that Freddie would be getting out of bed before Christmas. Or the Christmas after next for that matter.

Eventually, she left in a flurry of skirts, coats, car keys and hair, but no packed lunch. Connor yelled, "Your sandwich tin!" He raced to the kitchen, grabbed it from the fridge and ran after her, but she was already out of sight and he only just managed to jam his foot back inside the house to stop the front door from shutting him out.

Relieved to be back in the hall, Connor stared down at the tin. It had the initials 'G.L.M.' on the lid. He was pretty sure Mrs M's Christian name was Jeanette and you don't spell that with a 'G'. *Maybe it's the Irish spelling*, Connor thought, as he put the tin back in the fridge. After all, Freddie had told him, what sounds like 'Shivawn' is actually spelt 'Siobhan'. Crazy!

A minute later, and at the second attempt he perched awkwardly on the end of his friend's sickbed, after his first try had nearly crushed Freddie's feet. There were quite a few clothes scattered about the room and spilling out of half-opened drawers. It was much worse than Freddie's usual mess. Then

Connor noticed that next to his poster of the Solar System, Freddie had hung Uncle Patrick's dazzling Map of the World. It looked even more epic up on the wall than when they had unfurled it at the birthday party.

Freddie stared at Connor with exhausted, faraway eyes. Connor watched as a mysterious grin slowly spread across his friend's face, like the sun emerging from behind a dark cloud.

"W–what's b–been going on here, y'know … while I've b–been away?"

"Away?" Connor frowned. "What do you mean away?"

"I'll tell you in a minute. J–just fill me in on everything … since Sunday. Please?"

Connor's thoughts danced wildly as he tried to imagine where and what Freddie could have been doing since the party, and who with? He decided to bring him up to date with the most important piece of news (actually his only piece of news, apart from what it's like to sit silently in front of the telly in for four days eating flapjack).

"Met this weird lad called Kelvin in the park yesterday."

"And …?" Freddie rasped, letting his head fall back on to the pillow.

"He's just moved here and he asked me about school, so I told him it's alright. I nearly said,

30

'Except for Jasper,' but I didn't want to worry him because he was nervous enough already. He's got a real croaky voice and long greasy hair – and he was trying to carry two shopping bags and eat an ice cream. It was all going badly wrong."

Freddie smiled.

"Then he said, 'What's all this about some crazy boy called Freddie? This big lad, Jasper, told me he's a bit of a nutter.' Jasper told this Kelvin that people just pretend to like you. 'Especially the girls,' he said, but secretly they all think you're an idiot. It's not true, Freddie. He's just a new kid who ..." Connor didn't need to finish. It was just Jasper trying to turn the world against them. A long silence settled. But by the time Connor had thought of what he could say next, Freddie had drifted off to sleep again.

Connor stared at his best friend. Freddie was the youngest of a big Irish family that had moved to England ages ago, although he still had a very slight accent. Connor marvelled once again at the differences between Freddie and himself. Whereas Freddie was wiry, with chestnut brown hair and lively brown eyes, Connor was black haired and his frame was what he had heard a teacher once describe as 'generous'. And whereas Freddie's family were sparky and exciting, his own parents and brother were a collection of misfits who happened to share the same house and surname. It was all about as opposite as it could possibly get.

An hour later, with Freddie still dozing, Connor had studied every detail of the wonderful Map of the World over and over. He was now fidgety and bored and the room was hot and airless. He started making increasingly loud coughing noises in an attempt to wake Freddie up, which he eventually did.

"I ... I can't lie here all day. Let's go downstairs," Freddie whispered groggily.

Freddie sat down at the kitchen table opposite his friend and toyed with the salt cellar, transferring it thoughtfully from hand to hand.

"Connor ... You'll think I've gone mad. I don't know how to explain ... what's just happened to me."

Connor raised his eyebrows, "Why don't you try," he said gently.

Freddie nodded, then paused, seeming to collect his thoughts.

"We ... had a curry. Yesterday – Thursday! All sat around the patio table ... and Mum lit candles ... and Dad was telling some great stories. But by ten o'clock, I was really tired ... so I went up to bed. I just just managed to kick off my trainers ... and that was it. I fell asleep.

"I dreamt about this amazing palace ... I can't

remember where, but Uncle Patrick was in that stupid shirt, being a tour guide, talking rubbish. Then these freaky shadows began creeping in. Huge shadows ... like Jasper and Maz – but much older – grown up ... Then there was smoke everywhere. The shadows chased us and trapped us ... and Uncle Patrick started shouting weird old Irish stuff – and spinning about ... with his arms spread wide ... like he was trying to protect me.

"I knew I was dreaming, but I could actually feel Jasper slapping me ... It really hurt. And then ..."

Chapter Three

Freddie awoke with a massive jolt. He sat bolt upright, knocking the alarm clock off his bedside table. It teetered and fell, landing on the button that illuminated the digital display.

12:01 a.m. Was he still dreaming?

Freddie sat up. He felt a tremor of anticipation and then a crackle and surge of energy in his bedroom that made his eyes grow wide in alarm. From the silence of the rest of the house he started to hear something; music and voices swelling with increasing urgency, as they began swirling invisibly around him. Dozens of different people seemed to be talking in snippets of strange languages, like frenzied ghosts trying to impart crucial messages. Snatches of orchestras, rock bands, opera and bagpipes came and went, mixed chaotically with television and radio excerpts, as if someone was spinning a gigantic tuning dial. It was utterly bewildering. Freddie sat, open mouthed, trying to work out who was playing this trick on him. It wasn't some sort of birthday surprise, was it? If so, it was backfiring badly. He was scared stiff.

Light cut into the bedroom around the heavy curtains from the full moon outside, illuminating the wall opposite and the vivid colours of his majestic World Map. Freddie's gaze was drawn to India. He tried to look away, but it felt like his eyeballs were being dragged by magnets back towards the map. This was beyond freaky. All about him the tumult increased. The sounds were searing his eardrums and now there seemed to be a growing wind coursing around the room as well.

As Freddie continued to stare at the map, it suddenly started to pucker, showing the relief of cities, mountains and rivers. Freddie could not believe his eyes. His gaze was drawn upwards over the northern border India shared with Nepal. Completely against his will and with no control, his focus shot towards the capital, Kathmandu. Freddie blinked, trying to clear his head. He had to be seeing things, surely. The map appeared to be completely alive. Elephants and buses, people, planes, boats and trains sprang to life and began streaming across it, like ants in a forest. It was like his whole bedroom wall had become a vivid projection of the earth from the sky. It was alive. Freddie began backing away towards his pillows and clutched at the mattress.

Then, with a sudden and irresistible wrench, an unseen force ripped him away from his bed. He tried to hang on by clawing at the wooden headboard behind his pillow, but his body was stretched horizontally a foot above his duvet, which suddenly shot out from underneath him and joined the tornado of socks, pants and dirty washing dancing frantically around his room. Try as he might, he could not shift his gaze from Uncle Patrick's map. It appeared to have an absolute and unbreakable hold over him.

"Help! Stop it now! I've had enough. It's not funny any more. Dad! Mum! Stop it. Please!"

Now the map seemed to grow until it filled his entire field of vision. His eyes were drawn roughly eastwards, from Kathmandu to a place called Namche Bazaar, the letters of which dissolved, as tiny mountain tops thrust through the parchment in their place. Freddie's desperate last grip on the pine frame was broken and he hurtled towards the wall.

"No! Please ... No! Help!"

There was a thundering crack, like ice splitting on a frozen lake, as a huge tear appeared in the map. Beyond it, Freddie could see a tunnel; an endless vortex of swirling bright lights. The wall of his bedroom was melting and splitting, creating a gaping hole. The plaster and brickwork had become fluid.

"Help!" he tried to scream, but the sound was lost among a thousand other shouts. "Help me!" he cried again, but all the voices seemed to echo and mock him simultaneously. Freddie was speeding feet first towards the widening gap and it parted just enough to allow him through, accompanied by a truly deafening sound, as if a thousand sheets of paper were all torn at once.

He desperately tried to hang on to the jagged edge of the hole in his bedroom wall, but the bricks dissolved in his grasp.

Freddie was suddenly sucked into the mayhem of the tunnel beyond, with letters and numbers flashing past – left and right, above and below. As his velocity increased, Freddie began tumbling head over heels. He stretched out his arms to try to stabilise his body, but his hands sank into the walls, as if warping a plasma screen. Hundreds of pin-sharp images refracted and surged away from him as he thundered along. The vortex seemed to be simultaneously carrying him east, west, north, south, backwards, forwards and sideways through time. He knew he was awake, but he still had to be dreaming, surely. His mind froze with panic. How could he stop this living nightmare?

Hundreds of gigantic windows resembling cinema screens flashed past. Bursts of noise sounded with each different image. Choirs sang, comedians told punchlines, Roman armies shrieked as they battled, plane engines roared about him, all a piercing jangle of disjointed fragments. He sped past an image of his family last Christmas and even heard his Uncle Patrick shout out, "You're on your way boy. Remember, I'll always b ..." as a chorus of voices recited 'If—'. Then the interlude was lost amongst thundering horses' hooves and a trumpet fanfare from a medieval joust. Freddie was now giddy, seasick, car sick and, worst of all, tunnel sick.

"Help! What's happening? Why me?" he screamed out loud. "Aaarrrggghh!"

Freddie's thoughts tumbled about his brain like trainers in a washing machine. Then a fierce screeching sound filled the air and the tunnel began to judder. He finally seemed to be slowing down and could make out the individual scenes and the words and numbers zig-zagging through them. What looked like a trench from the First World War flashed by, just as a huge shell exploded, throwing mud and debris in the air. It was so realistic Freddie ducked, throwing his hands up to protect himself.

By the time he felt brave enough to look again, a baying crowd in a Parisian square surrounded a guillotine, begging for another head to join the pile in the groaning basket. This was replaced by a desperate man crawling in a shredded and bloody uniform across a vast desert landscape, with no sign of shade or water. Freddie tore his gaze away and the bombardment which had scorched his ears gradually subsided. He was coming to a furious halt, as if riding on a speeding tube train as the brakes suddenly slammed on.

Finally, with a few jerks and a deafening series of crunches just like a lorry makes when it changes gear, Freddie shuddered to a standstill beside a truly magical vista. It spread fast from its position on his right, like fluid escaping a mould. It flowed over his head and around his feet, quickly joining together on his left at about shoulder height to fully surround him. The last few numbers fluttered down and set solidly by his feet. There was a '17', two 'I's and a '9', in front of an '89'. He had no idea what they meant and he was too shattered to care.

There was silence.

And Freddie's world had completely changed.

Two minutes before, he had been asleep in his safe, comfortable bedroom. Now, he was on a small grassy hillock shielding his eyes from bright sunlight above a beautiful semi-circular village. The settlement clung to the side of a steep valley amongst the highest mountains he had ever seen in his life. The view was dominated by massive snow-topped peaks, tumbling into blue-grey glaciers. These in turn gave way to impossibly sheer, wooded valley sides that spilled ferocious, bubbling torrents of meltwater onto unseen valley floors.

Freddie was so stunned, he completely forgot to breathe. He took a huge gulp of air, but however hard he tried he couldn't seem to get enough oxygen into his lungs. He felt a new, even greater surge of terror. It was a horrible sensation. Freddie was gasping for breath and flopped sideways onto the sparse, coarse grass.

He closed his eyes and tried to make it all go away. What had just happened to him? Where was he? What was that tunnel all about? Why had his parents done this to him? It was the worst birthday surprise he could think of ... Ever! Maybe it wasn't them. Maybe it was spies, or some foreign gangster organisation after his ... his *what*? Why would anyone want to do this to *him*? He had nothing anyone would want to steal. Uncle Patrick's map was totally ruined; with a massive split down the middle. What *had* just happened? Maybe his mum and dad would know. Or Uncle Patrick. Would they call the police? What could *they* do? *What if I can't get home again?*

He opened his eyes to try to stop the millions of unanswerable questions swarming around his battered brain and surveyed the landscape before him.

"Oh, wow!" he whispered. Then again, slightly louder, "Wow!"

He really did seem to be somewhere completely different, although it still looked like Planet Earth. Freddie didn't need to pinch himself to know he was awake, because every part of his body was aching and sore. He had to get his act together quickly. He knew these first few moments in his new surroundings were vital. He'd heard a survival man on the telly saying so as he'd skinned a rabbit and made a shelter out of branches and leaves.

Freddie had to be at an enormous altitude for the air to be this thin. This theory was borne out by the dramatic scenery. He took tiny, regular breaths. Good. It was working. He felt calmer.

Now. Think. THINK!

Far below him, only one settlement stood out. It was the horseshoe shaped village he had first seen, perched on the edge of a cliff, beyond which there was nothing but a deep chasm. The village was shaped like an amphitheatre. It was laid out in six or seven curved horizontal streets, which looked like giant steps climbing up the hillside. "Where on earth am I?" Freddie wondered. "Just because I zoomed through the map into Nepal ... doesn't mean that's where I actually am now." He had to admit though, that the scenery did seem to fit.

Freddie became aware of how bitingly cold it was. He only had on his baggy jeans, sweatshirt and thin, hooded fleece. Even that had just been a lucky last minute addition whilst eating the birthday curry in the garden. He shuddered as the cold got to his bones, and tried to focus. He ticked off the things he was absolutely certain of on his very cold fingers.

1. He was high up, outside a mountain village, in a far-off country.

2. It was freezing, even in the strong sunshine.

3. Every move was an effort, so he would have to conserve his energy. He really needed to get warm and find somewhere to shelter. And …

4. He had no shoes on!

"*No way!*" he exclaimed, wasting valuable breath.

This was a disaster. Even though he had his thick white training socks on, he could already feel his toes going numb, and this spurred him into action. Freddie stood up and staggered like Uncle Patrick had done at Mollie's wedding as a consequence of drinking too much champagne and trying to dance with the bridesmaids. A breeze picked up and swirled the grass at his side. Freddie turned and saw for the first time the view behind him. He was speechless. Far in the distance were mountains so high it was like looking at the roof of the world.

Not obvious at first, Freddie now spotted a plateau amongst the peaks, with a beautiful building like a palace at its centre. Miniscule reflections from the windows sparkled in the sunlight. Beyond this was an unforgettable sight; a mountain top Freddie knew he recognised.

Surely it was Mount Everest. It had to be. Its beautiful pyramid-shaped summit marked the highest point on Earth. It was an image Freddie knew well from a project they'd done at school to mark the 65th anniversary of the first men to climb the mountain.

Amidst all sorts of useless trivia, the numbers 8,850 and 29,035 revolved round on imaginary drums in Freddie's head, clicking into place like a fruit machine bringing up a row of lemons. 8,850 was Everest's height in metres, and 29,035 was its remarkable total in feet. Over five miles high.

It was first successfully summitted by Edmund Hillary and Sherpa Tensing Norgay in 1953. To celebrate the 65th anniversary, Freddie's class had been in contact via email with an expedition that year. He had longed to see Everest for himself and pay tribute to the brave climbers that had tried and failed so many times, as well as the lucky ones that had succeeded. Was this his birthday present from his parents then? Somehow transporting him to Everest? "Don't be an idiot!" he said to himself. "How could they have done that?"

Then a new feeling of dread entered his thoughts as he gazed at the most talked about piece of rock on Earth. One of his project chapter headings had been 'One in Ten'. Freddie grimly remembered what he had written.

One in ten people die on the high slopes of Everest.

One in ten perish on the freezing icy flanks, or fall, or run out of oxygen.

One in ten simply exhaust their energy and lose the will to live.

Freddie was already losing the feeling in his feet and he had been there only a few minutes. He must get warm and he must get shoes. But from where?

He started down the dusty path away from the small hillock, which was the most direct route to the village that lay thousands of feet below. The ground was intensely cold. During pauses for breath he scanned his surroundings for shelter. He was excited, amazed, and terrified all at once.

"I've got to find out what's happening, why I'm here, and how I can get home again." He shiverered and whispered on the breeze, "Time to get warm. Everest isn't going anywhere … and I want to stay alive to see it."

Chapter Four

In the kitchen of 10 Normandy Avenue, Connor stared wide-eyed at his friend and tried to rank the thousand or so questions he wanted to ask in order of importance. Freddie had stopped his tale abruptly, suddenly realising how weird it was to be back at home, telling Connor about this amazing adventure from the other side of the world. He coughed, rubbed the sores on his face, sighed and closed his eyes. The spell was temporarily broken.

"Shall I make the soup?" Connor suggested, hoping that Freddie would carry on if he felt stronger. Freddie nodded, watching Connor reach in the open fridge and move the battered sandwich tin to one side.

Freddie gasped and staggered to his feet. "Oh! Brilliant, Connor, I can't believe it! The tin ... It's here! It's safe."

"What? This old thing?" Connor shook it.

"Don't please!" Freddie yelled. "Be gentle. Give it to me please ... You just won't believe the things I've done to keep hold of this. I'll tell you about it later. If I go to that part of the story now, I'll miss out loads of other stuff and it won't make any sense. I must have ... I must have put it in the fridge last night, when I got back – to keep it cold. I don't know why. I'm going mad! I really am going ..." His tired voice trailed off.

Connor passed him the tin carefully. Freddie cradled it and smiled. He sat down and rested his head on his arms, staring at the battered object on the table in front of him. Then the phone shattered the silence. Connor was torn. The last thing he wanted was to answer it. What he needed was a thousand quick answers from Freddie, but he pressed answer and listened to Freddie's mum.

"Yes, Freddie's feeling a lot better, Mrs M. I've just made his lunch," he told her.

"Thank you, Connor. You're a darlin' boy," she said. "I'll be back just before five o'clock, but I haven't cancelled the doctor's appointment yet. I want to see him myself before I do. Has he said anything to you, Connor? About what started it all off? It can't have been the curry because both his dad and I are fine."

Connor blurted a few unrelated and unconvincing noises. His thoughts were so frazzled, he just couldn't concentrate on anything she was saying.

But thankfully Mrs M cut him off. "How did he get those nasty wee marks on his face, I wonder? They're not burns are they, Connor? Has he said anything about them?

"No, Mrs M. No. I don't think they're burns. No."

Mrs M seemed a little happier after Connor's mumbled reassurances. When he returned to the kitchen, he found Freddie sitting bolt upright, his lunch untouched, so Connor decided to try a spoonful of the soup before it went cold, and a small piece of the bread.

Freddie took one or two deep breaths as if deciding where to pick up the story, whilst Connor sat quietly savouring the fantastic flavour of the soup. *Just one more spoonful*, he thought. Freddie toyed with the mysterious tin box and stared at the initials.

Two minutes later, Connor looked down to see an empty bowl. He pulled a face and looked over awkwardly at his friend, but Freddie just smiled, shrugged off a shiver, scratched his forehead and carried on telling his story.

"Shoes. I knew I needed shoes or I wasn't going to last long against the cold ..."

Freddie bent over to look at his feet and felt something sharp digging into his thigh. Money! It was the change from the takeaway. He had well over six pounds. But what good would English money be in Nepal, if indeed this was Nepal? And then he thought back to the map. What if this was actually Namche Bazaar? Wasn't bazaar another name for a market? Markets always sell shoes.

Freddie's breathing seemed to improve the further he scrambled down the hill. He stopped every few minutes to massage his feet and warm them. Then he spotted a low stone hut off to his right. He checked for signs of life. This was his first glimpse of anywhere that could possibly be used as an emergency shelter. He sat on a large boulder opposite for five minutes with his socks off, pretending to attend to some imaginary blisters. The window was tightly shuttered and there was no sign of anyone.

Suddenly, he heard the scraping of heavy hooves on the rocky path behind him. He turned and saw a line of huge, shaggy beasts snaking down the mountain, all carrying immense loads. They had boxes, bags and all sorts strapped to their backs. They were like large highland cows, except hairier, and a whole lot scarier too. They had wild eyes and huge horns sprouting in great long curves from the sides of their heads.

"Yaks!" Freddie said out loud, as if answering a question in Uncle Patrick's Christmas Quiz. He climbed higher onto the boulder to get away from the beasts as they descended the treacherous path. The first one gave him a suspicious glare and a stringy, wet snort as its huge hooves shuddered on the rocky path. The tricky surface would be difficult enough for a climber with proper boots, let alone an animal weighing a ton and laden with equipment. The second and third in the line had passed him now. Obviously, a glare and a stringy wet snort was the traditional welcome from a yak; all three had done the same thing.

So far they had all had very matted, dark brown coats, but the fourth was brown with dirty creamy bits and the fifth was black. The sixth, another brown one, hadn't seen Freddie on his rocky perch. When it turned its head and caught sight of him it reacted with surprise, staggering sideways and sending shards of splintered stone into the undergrowth. The yak soon regained its footing, but it had spooked the others, as well as Freddie. Just then, he heard a call from the back of the line. The voice was high and musical, full of strength and reassurance.

The last of the yaks filed past, calmer now after the soothing words from their driver. Freddie was amazed to see that the voice belonged to a young girl of about his own age, dressed in faded, well-worn, shapeless layers. She was weighed down by the biggest load he had ever seen a human being carry. Not only was there a full-sized rucksack on her back, a second load was suspended from a wide cloth band wrapped around her forehead. It sat on the top of the backpack, causing her to lean forward to counteract the enormous weight.

The girl had the most beautiful face he thought he had ever seen in his life. Her eyes were full of kindness and she laughed and chattered with her yaks, appearing to gently mock them for their panic. She too was surprised when she saw Freddie. He was trying hard to blend in with his surroundings, but he actually looked like an awkward teenager in the wrong clothes, in the wrong place, at the wrong time. But the girl didn't seem fazed that a strangely dressed, barefoot boy was perched on a rock. She treated Freddie to a broad grin.

"Namaste," she said, smiling. Freddie was in no doubt that this was a greeting of some sort. "Na–mas–te," she repeated, in three equal syllables. Before he knew it, Freddie had shouted it back, unnecessarily loud, in rather a croaky voice.

"Na–mas–te."

What was even more embarrassing was that at the same time, Freddie automatically waved his left hand, which held one of his socks. The girl laughed at the sight of the off-white object fluttering in the morning breeze. She wobbled sideways slightly, adjusting the broad headband of her top pack, before balancing again and continuing her journey.

Freddie stared bleakly at the receding yaks, but

more truthfully he was looking at their driver. All too quickly they had passed by and were gone. The only consolation was that he seemed to have learnt a word. 'Namaste.'

"Progress from ten minutes ago," he smiled, trying to look on the bright side. Although he had to admit, waving a dirty, shredded sock was not a good start and could hardly have impressed the gorgeous girl.

He took another look at the hut opposite, now certain that it was unoccupied. It would make a brilliant shelter for the night once he had found some shoes. Freddie decided that if he doubled the top of his sock back over his heel and toes, he could protect his feet better and move a lot quicker, chasing the train of hairy yaks and their driver. He could not stop thinking about 'Namaste', as he'd decided to call her, carrying the impossible load and bent into a light breeze that played with wisps of her jet black hair.

Half an hour later he crested a ridge and a tiny plateau came into sight. Freddie saw 'Namaste' cross to a stream, where she let her beasts drink the tumbling mountain meltwater. He felt strangely light-headed again, but for a different reason.

As he approached, he heard her echoing voice singing unselfconsciously. She was dressed in simple old clothes; threadbare and colourless. Her only luxury appeared to be a pair of battered plimsolls, which she removed, along with her socks. However Freddie's adventure was going to turn out, it had definitely taken an unexpected and happier twist in the last hour. 'Namaste' caught sight of him and, with a broad grin on her face, waved one of her socks at Freddie. Freddie burst out laughing, calling 'Namaste' as he continued past her. Then, all too soon, she was out of sight once again.

Freddie soon came upon a sign in beautiful swirly writing and, below it, an English translation:

WELCUM TO NAMCHE BAZAAR,
SHERPA CAPTAL OF THE WORLD,
ALTITUDE 3,450 MERTEES.

So he was in Nepal. But what on earth was he doing here and how was he going to get home?

All of the tiny houses of Namche Bazaar were made of stone and wood, with roofs of slate or corrugated iron. He noticed some small brown patties on rounded rocks beside the path. They looked like hamburgers, being dried in the heat of the now considerable sun. Freddie's stomach rumbled. He would have loved to eat one, but decided it would probably be missed. None of the buildings in the narrow streets were more than two storeys high. They had long strips of multi-coloured flags strung between them, similar to those he had seen fluttering on the surrounding hillsides.

He could see what looked like a market in a clearing

by the very edge of the cliff, but the tiny street that led there was packed, and not just with people. Little shops spilled their contents, which collided with the overflowing produce of the shops opposite. Dogs, cats, goats, chickens, children, climbers, locals and sherpas all jammed the narrow lane.

Freddie stood self-consciously, pushing his hands hard into his pockets, forcing his baggy jeans down to hide as much of his feet as possible. Taking a deep breath and wishing himself luck, he set off in search of footwear.

What first caught his eye was a shop selling post-cards, mostly featuring Mount Everest. The picture he liked best was taken at sunset, and written underneath was: *Sagarmatha, Chomolangma, Mt Everest 29,028 ft (8,848 metres).* As Freddie stared at the well-thumbed card, something started niggling at him.

He knew the Nepalese called Everest 'Sagarmatha', so he supposed 'Chomolangma' must be what the Tibetans called it. But it was the height that concerned him. Surely Everest wasn't getting any shorter? He thought the highest point on Earth was 29,035 ft (8,850 meters), which meant that the altitude on the postcard was wrong.

Then something clicked. Freddie gazed at the postcard with renewed confusion and more than a hint of fear. Everest's height had been recalibrated about twenty years ago. That meant he must now be in Nepal at least twenty years before the time he left home. This would explain the slightly old-fashioned clothes people were wearing. Not only had the vortex brought him half way across the world, it had spun him back through time as well. He felt suddenly very scared but quickly tried to supress the emotion. It wouldn't help him find shoes and shelter. And why he had been deposited here was still a total mystery. What could he possibly have done to bring it all upon himself? Such things only happened in books or films. There was no use even thinking about it. He didn't have any useful answers just yet.

Then a flash of colour caught his eye as a gaggle of small children made their way past. They ranged from wobbling, wide-eyed toddlers to smiling older children, all dressed in what looked like hand-me-down clothes. The older children carried the contented youngsters, who pointed and giggled at huge, bearded mountaineers, with their bulging rucksacks and walking poles. The only toys they carried were marbles, with which the older children began to play an uncomplicated game. The tiny ones shadowed their brothers and sisters, either clinging to their sides, or wrapped cleverly with a shawl and carried on their backs; little human backpacks, in a sea of huge mountain rucksacks.

Freddie stood observing the game from the shaded verandah of an empty shop. One of the smallest girls, dressed in a faded pink cardigan and no older than three, stood staring at Freddie. She returned his friendly waves.

"Namaste," Freddie said to the girl. She hid behind her brother's back, peeping out to see if Freddie was still looking, which of course he was.

As she popped her head out, he waved again, repeating, "Namaste." Her face erupted with pleasure. She looked like she was considering replying, but instead darted back to safety. Twice more she and Freddie repeated the moves before finally she mouthed a tiny, "Namaste."

Freddie felt triumphant. Now that she had started, there was no stopping the little girl, and each time she emerged she was bolder with her cries.

The fun only stopped when two men, one smoking a very large and pungent cigar, pushed past her, almost knocking her to the ground and scattering the children's marbles with a crunch of heavy walking boots. The spell was completely broken. The tiny girl revolved on the spot, following the intruders with a baleful gaze. She coughed at the strong smoke from the cigar. Her friends picked up their trodden marbles, staring forlornly at the surly pitch invaders.

Freddie moved on, sad that the contact had been broken. He looked back, managing to catch her eye one last time and waved goodbye. As she waved in return, Freddie smiled. He was improving. For the first time today, he had waved at someone without a sock in his hand.

He continued downhill, passing a small neat building that turned out to be a bank offering currency exchange. A queue waited patiently in gentle conversation on the shaded side of the street. The other side was bathed in bright sunshine, adding a certain appeal to the goods on offer. Freddie presumed it would change in the afternoon as the sun went over, and then the shops, which were now shaded, would have their turn in the limelight. Freddie decided that Namche Bazaar felt like a place where things worked out for the best and he smiled to himself.

But right at that particular moment, all hell broke loose.

Chapter Five

A rumbling wall of noise erupted from the top of the street. Freddie felt the ground tremble. All he could see was a cloud of dust, as if a house had collapsed. It took him a moment to realise it was the thunder of hooves. People began jumping out of the way. Fruit, postcards, clothes, rucksacks and cameras flew through the air, abandoned by diving figures. The terrifying cause was a runaway train of huge, hairy, charging yaks.

Freddie recorded all of this in the turn of his head and the blink of an eye as the beasts rampaged down the steep street towards him. Screams and shouts rang out in many languages – desperate calls for help and snatched warnings of impending disaster. Then a sickening thought hit Freddie: *What about the children?* He looked for them amidst the panic, but legs, bodies, hats, bags and equipment criss-crossed his path. People shouted for him to run to safety, but he fought his way back through the chaos.

The clamour of the hooves grew louder. His route cleared and Freddie spied the little girl in the pink cardigan, standing motionless in the middle of the street about ten metres ahead of him. Her brother tried to scoop her up, but he was hoisted away by a huge, khaki-clad tourist, inadvertently removing the girl's only hope of rescue.

There was now no one between the yaks and the girl, and no one between the girl and Freddie. He was her only chance. The rampaging beasts were closing quickly. The girl stood crying, looking for help, sensing that the noise and panic spelled imminent danger.

Freddie sprung into action. Although he was nearer to the girl than the beasts, it was a rapidly closing gap and it was a struggle up the hill wearing only his socks.

Everything jerked on, frame-by-frame, like a series of staged photographs. Hooves, shrieks, dust, debris, screams, scrapes and snorts packed into a few metres of the tiny street; a tiny street, in a small hill town, in a country far away, in a lost moment of time.

Maybe *this* was why he was here! Suddenly it all made sense. This was Freddie's moment. A vision of a smiling Uncle Patrick flashed through his mind.

He ran with all his might, as the yaks charged with all their strength. Freddie accelerated, pushing himself to the limit of his capabilities. He swooped as if picking up a cricket ball and grabbed the wailing infant by the cardigan. He hauled her close to his chest, already moving sideways and diving for cover. As he did so, the first of the hooves shattered the glass of the abandoned marbles. The yaks roared past, leaving a trail of devastation in their wake. It was like a hurricane passing through – a hurricane of hairy beasts, with long, thick, matted hair and horns sharper than daggers.

Even when they had passed, the roar of chaos continued – less intense now as the luckier people lower down had more time to get out of the way. Finally, the yaks slowed and some shopkeepers in the distance even had time to haul some of their produce inside to save it from damage.

A silence descended. Gradually people began to stir from their places of safety, checking their own and other people's injuries.

For Freddie, it was very different. He lay completely still.

With the tiny girl gripped safely in his arms, he had thrown himself through the air like a goalkeeper saving a penalty and landed on the raised verandah of the empty shop. The girl in the pink cardigan had been deposited in the copious khaki lap of a large lady trekker. Freddie had hit the rough stone wall with a sickening thud. He took the main force on his shoulder, but with enough impact on his head to temporarily knock himself out. The next thing he knew, he was being pinched.

When his eyes shot open, he found himself looking

at six huge identical khaki-clad lady tourists, rotating anticlockwise around a massive central version of the same woman. The pinching continued.

"Hey! Stop it!" Freddie protested, as the six rotating women gradually merged into a single, khaki vision that shrieked at him in a heavy American accent, "Hey! Kid. Listen ... you're a hero! You saved this little peanut! You're a reg–u–lar Superman!"

Each accolade was accompanied by a painful little tweak of Freddie's skin as she leaned closer to him. Freddie pulled away. He felt his bruised head with one hand and began to examine his bleeding feet with the other, removing what remained of his socks.

Out of the corner of his eye he caught sight of a now much dirtier pink cardigan and, above it, a beaming smile. The tiny girl held her brother's hand and stood safely by his side as if nothing had happened. She looked at Freddie, ducked behind her brother, waited a second or two, shot back out smiling and exclaimed, "Na–mas–te."

All Freddie's pain disappeared. He waved his hand, which, he remembered too late, held his socks and he laughed out of relief and exhaustion. He became aware of the great fuss around him and thought he saw his Uncle Patrick walking away down the hill, but his vision was still slightly blurred and it could have been anyone. The girl's parents arrived and offered some heartfelt thanks. The colossal American and her party snapped away with cameras and retold the heroic deeds of the small boy.

"Ahm tellin' you, that child's a he–ro."

A large crowd had gathered in a semi-circle in front of the shop and now only Freddie, the girl, her brother and grateful parents were on the verandah. People smiled and clapped and began singing an impromptu song, which the Nepalese in the crowd swirled and danced to in a dusty circle.

'Resham–fee–ree–ree,' it sounded like. 'Resham–fee–ree–ree.'

Freddie was relieved to see the tourists turn their cameras onto the locals and was about to slip away unnoticed, when a hush descended on the crowd. It parted to allow a young girl through. The singing was replaced by angry shouts as Freddie watched 'Namaste' walk along what had become a terrible tunnel of shame. Insults were being hurled by people who knew the yaks to be hers. She looked at the ground as she walked slowly down the hill, trying to get to where her disgraced charges had eventually been stopped and tethered. Some of the shopkeepers added their fury to the throng, clearly upset at the loss of their stock and demanding something be done.

Namaste stopped in front of the boarded-up shop where the bulk of the crowd were gathered. She tried to explain events in bursts of sobbing Nepalese. On noting the many blank and bewildered faces of the climbers and trekkers staring back, she repeated her confession in stilted English.

"I ... I sorry. But, big rock–full – *no!* rock–*fall* on road, up long way there. I ... I ... so sorry. The rock ... he frighten ... my yaks. He cause big problem and *strut* ... no! start ... start to ... stram ... *no!*"

"Stampede," interjected a knight in shining armour in the form of Freddie Malone. He stood and looked supportively at 'Namaste'.

"Yes. Thank you sir ... *stam*–pee." She flicked a small smile of thanks in his direction.

"They stampee and run ... loose their loads, and I have no help – just me."

Freddie held out a hand for Namaste to join him on the verandah. She took his outstretched palm, which still held his blood-stained socks. She gave him a baffled look as she stepped up onto the platform. Freddie stood beside her with his head bowed, not thinking about yaks or lifesaving but, instead, what an idiot he was for sticking out his right hand, which contained socks, instead of his left, which didn't.

'Namaste' continued in her native tongue and gradually the crowd's attitude towards her began to change. They explained to her what had happened, culminating in Freddie's dramatic dash and the split-second rescue. 'Namaste' glanced round to gasp at Freddie. She had her hands over her mouth and was crying again now with large, shoulder shaking sobs.

She could see the scale of the damage caused and the level of danger several dozen people, but especially this strange sock-waving boy, had been through on her behalf.

The crowd parted again for a thin and frail old man who was being led gently by an equally old, but far less frail lady. She shepherded the ancient man's every step, quietly soothing her partner with regular encouragement. A low murmur rippled around the now mainly local onlookers. The tourists were drifting away, rightly feeling they were intruding. Even the colossal American lady had left in a swirl of khaki fabric, barking to her companions, "How am I gonna get all this in my journal guys?"

The sobbing Namaste approached the elderly couple. She bowed and repeated all she'd just heard, at the end of which she turned and indicated to Freddie. The ancient couple moved towards him. The tiny old man proudly shook off the helping arms of his wife and stood as upright as he could manage before the crowd. He spoke in husky tones and he gesticulated wildly as he spoke. Freddie wished he would stay still. Every time the man flung an arm out to emphasise something, he swayed dramatically and had to be steadied. Occasionally he was interrupted by people, but he seemed to answer their questions with a rattling sentence or two. His manner was proud and unapologetic, but it seemed to strike just the right note with everyone.

A group of men led the now immaculately behaved yaks back up the street, collecting the spilt baggage as they went. The last of the huge beasts looked at Freddie and honoured him with a wet, stringy snort.

The traders were given various notes in compensation under the instruction of the old man and out of the purse of the old woman. All accepted their settlement and walked away satisfied.

Freddie was still feeling terrible, but with 'Namaste' so close, he was content to just sit back and observe. Although, he made absolutely sure his socks were firmly hidden in his pocket, to avoid any more unscheduled appearances.

Freddie halted his tale once again and looked at Connor. His top lip curled into the beginning of a smile just as the front door opened and Mrs M filled the hall, loaded down with shopping bags. They were brimming full of medicines and vitamins, cold cures and potions – every remedy under the sun, including the one guaranteed method of returning Freddie to full fitness, his favourite pick-me-up: sausages!

Chapter Six

Sausages, mashed potato and garden peas. Not frozen or even fresh peas; they had to be a specific brand of tinned peas that sloshed around in a sweet, green juice. Freddie's special ritual then traditionally involved sculpting a 'mash mountain', pouring the peas over the top and letting the pea juice soak into the potato. Combined with the flavour of the sausages and strong English mustard, it was Freddie's idea of heaven. It always made him feel better.

Standing in the doorway with shopping bags, handbag, door keys, car keys, raincoat, evening paper and the correct brand of tinned garden peas, Mrs M could not help but pause Freddie's story. Connor sprung to his feet and tried to help, but they both got into a massive tangle.

"Thanks for trying, Connor, darlin', but I'll be

quicker under my own steam."

Freddie put on a brave face, "I'm fine now, Mum, you can cancel the doctor."

Mrs M looked at him for a long moment before nodding.

"Okay," she said. "Thank you, Connor, for looking after him. You're a treasure, but I think Freddie's had enough excitement for now. Yous two can catch up again tomorrow."

"Oh! Okay ... No problem, Mrs M," Connor nodded, somewhat reluctantly.

"Let's meet at ten o'clock in the park. Should be too early for Jasper to be looking for any trouble," Freddie said, showing his friend to the front door.

"Okay. See you then – by the swings?" Connor fist-bumped Freddie and headed home.

Connor walked slowly away from Freddie's house, not wanting the incredible day to end and battling to make sense of all Freddie had told him so far. He kept wondering what great mystery was still to be revealed. What about the box in the fridge? Had Freddie been in Nepal to save the small girl in the pink cardigan? If so, it was job done ... and why did Uncle Patrick keep popping up?

As Freddie looked forward to his special supper, Connor trudged back to his house, where adventures only happened on the televisions that were permanently on in the corner of the lounge, kitchen and bedrooms, whether anyone was watching them or not.

He stared at the shop windows in their grey stretch of the high street. Then, as if his eyes were being pulled by a magnet, he was inevitably drawn to the newsagents, McKenzie's. As he was surveying the awesome Pick 'n' Mix display, suddenly a harsh voice cut in.

"What you doin', fat boy."

Connor froze. There, clustered around him, were the last people he wanted to see; Jasper and his minions – Maz, Rowan and Paul. With all the shops already shut for the evening, there was no one about to help.

Connor dropped his head, any kind of response deserting him. There was no point in saying anything anyway. Jasper grabbed Connor by the hair. His piercing blue eyes drilling into the bigger boy's face.

"What you creeping about here for, eh?" he spat. "You've been creeping about all holiday. No teachers around here to help you now are there, fat boy?"

Connor shrugged. He'd learned that answering back always seemed to make things worse. The usual ritual of him being pushed from one to the other started up and gathered momentum. They all laughed and jeered at their large, spongy target.

"Yeah! Connor, you great bouncy castle!"

Connor knew Jasper would probably jab in a punch the next time he was propelled the bully's way. As the insults grew louder, the shoving increased. Connor tried to blank it all out. Today, in Freddie's company, he had been transported to such an amazing place and heard about such wonderful people. The contrast with his present company was almost funny.

Connor fixed his mind elsewhere as the taunts continued. He was high on a mountain track amongst glaciers and ice walls. In the distance he saw Namche Bazaar, and walking towards him was Freddie with the girl in the pink cardigan proudly carried on a freshly groomed yak led by 'Namaste'. All smiling, they waved and called out, "Connor," their clothes rippling as they bounded towards him in slow motion, on a warm, sweet-smelling breeze.

And then came Jasper's special delivery.

Connor doubled over as Jasper's right fist caught him in the flesh that covered the bottom of his ribs. His only consolation was that it would hurt someone else a lot more, as the band of natural padding he had was there to soak it up.

"I owe you that. You made me miss my cricket!" hissed Jasper.

As the pain surged through his body, Connor felt his eyes prickle with tears. Maz had grabbed both his arms from behind and was ready to shove him back Jasper's way. Connor heard himself begging and whimpering. He knew he would now do or say anything if it meant bringing the torture to an end.

Suddenly, a car horn blasting out furiously at the traffic lights made the gang stop and stare in alarm. By the time Mr M had extricated himself from his seat belt and jumped out of the car, screaming for Jasper to stay where he was, the attackers had fled in different directions.

Mr M put an arm around Connor and led him to his Saab, shouting at the van driver behind who was complaining about the hold up.

"For the love of God, man! Can you not see this boy's hurt? Use your eyes, you eejit!"

Mr Malone slammed the car door and accelerated away from the lights with a good amount of wheel-spin.

"Are you all right, Connor? I tell ya, it's a good job my brother Paddy isn't here. There wouldn't be a paving stone left unturned between here and the sewer where those lowlifes come from. Do ya know them?"

"Nuh," Connor lied, shaking his head, then he wiped away the remaining tears and looked out at the passing streets. He thanked the still fuming Mr Malone as he was dropped off at the top of his road, grateful it wasn't directly outside his house, so he had time to get himself together before going in. He straightened his clothes, trying to think of something cheerful to say in case he bumped into anyone in the hall. He needn't have bothered. No one batted an eyelid.

Connor spotted a chicken pie and some oven chips by the microwave. It was his usual cue not to disturb anyone and just help himself. From the clinking of cutlery coupled with the slightly rude, farting noise that squeezing a plastic tomato ketchup bottle makes, it sounded like his mum, dad and elder brother were already eating theirs in the lounge in front of the telly.

Connor reached up for a plate and felt a surge of pain from his bruised ribs. He yelped and decided he'd better have a few extra chips for being so brave.

Freddie rang on the land line an hour or so later, saying he couldn't talk for long because he was being sent to bed for an early night.

"My dad told me what happened. Do you still feel like meeting up tomorrow? There's plenty more to tell you, Connor. Y'know, about the box and stuff ..."

Connor heard Freddie's mum call out that anything else could wait till the morning.

"Yeah! I'll be there, but what about the box?" Connor asked. But Freddie's time was up.

"Gotta go. See you tomorrow," he said, and he

was gone.

Connor dragged himself upstairs, past all the spaces where he would put pictures of family events and great places, if his family ever did anything or had any experiences worth remembering and framing.

He closed his bedroom door, lay on his bed, closed his eyes and thought of Namaste, and the next thing he knew, it was Saturday morning.

Chapter Seven

Connor's belly and ribs were both hurting, but for different reasons. His ribs had a good excuse after the jabs from Jasper, but his stomach-ache was purely self inflicted. He had eaten far more than he should have done when he'd got home and then fallen asleep in an awkward position. It felt like the pie and chips had formed a huge immovable wodge in his tummy.

Great! he thought. Freddie lies on his bed fully clothed and flies off to Nepal. I do the same and end up with gut ache! He drank two pints of water in quick succession, hoping to shift the blockage. Pleased with the effect, he decided he'd better have a couple of slices of toast and jam to see him though the morning.

Grunted goodbyes followed, and he was out of the door long before he needed to be, giving him plenty of time to wander up the high street to the top end of town for the ten o'clock rendezvous. The sky was a clear blue and Connor could already feel the warmth in the air and the promise of a perfect summer's day.

As he neared the park swings next to the dried up concrete paddling pool, he saw Kelvin sitting on a bench. Connor decided to join him.

"Y'alright," the scruffy kid croaked nervously. He offered Connor a piece of a chocolate bar he was close to finishing, making a real mess trying to divide it.

Connor took the lump cautiously. "Thanks." He let his love of chocolate overcome any worries of being poisoned and swallowed the piece of lukewarm gunge in one.

"I got no one to hang out with 'ere," Kelvin mused, staring out across the empty park. "I had loads of mates where I used to live. I tried Jasper and them for a bit, but that was rubbish coz I was ordered about the whole time. They made me do all the things none of the others would. What's the point of that?" He shrugged and continued, "Jasper said, to be a full gang member, you gotta steal somethin' from a shop, or find out something we're not supposed to know, or infil–som'ink ... infil–tate Freddie's gang of lunatics and become a double agent."

Kelvin uttered Jasper's last option warily. Connor couldn't help but feel slightly sorry for him. "If you don't know a secret, why don't you make one up? It'd be easy. Jasper will never find out whether it's true or not. But joining Jasper's gang's probably not a great thing to do anyway. They're total idiots. They did this to me yesterday."

Connor lifted his t-shirt and showed Kelvin the two blossoming purple bruises under his ribs. Kelvin gasped. "Oo–urgh! Look at them!"

Connor suddenly felt rather proud and slightly important. He decided to show off a little more.

"Freddie's my best friend. He's great and he's just been on a real adventure. He's been telling me all about it. He's got this tin. It's really important. It's full of, well, I promised Freddie I wouldn't tell anyone. But it's really special. He's let me look in it of course." Connor stopped, digesting his own words. Why was he lying? Why was he trying to impress Kelvin? And what had he just done?

Kelvin looked around nervously, "I gotta, y'know, see my ... and get the whassisnames for the thingy," he stammered.

Connor shouted after him. "Don't listen to Jasper. It won't do you any good!"

Kelvin nodded shiftily and walked away quickly. Connor watched him head for the high street, glancing back at the swings every so often.

Connor suddenly felt sick at what he'd revealed to Kelvin. "You stupid, stupid idiot," he said to himself quietly, shaking his head.

As the church clock struck ten, Freddie entered the park through the gates on the opposite side, picking up the pace when he saw Connor. He sat down carefully on the next swing, obviously still feeling a little battered and bruised himself. His face was still blotchy and blistered and he had new plasters on some of his fingers.

"Sorry about Jasper, mate," he said quietly, shaking his head.

Connor shrugged modestly. "It was nothing, really. Didn't hurt that much." For the second time in ten minutes he had lied and for the second time in ten minutes, he showed off his bruises.

"Wow!" Freddie whispered. "It must've hurt, they're huge!"

"Nah, they're not too bad."

They moved away from the swings and settled on the bench at the far end of the empty paddling pool. It had a good strategic view of most of the park and was protected from behind by some dense shrubs. They stood a fair chance of being able to spot Jasper early if he was out looking for trouble. Freddie carefully placed his bulging rucksack between his feet. Then sat in silence.

"So?" Connor prompted.

His friend smiled patiently.

"Yeah, let me think. Where were we?"

Connor rattled out the last few major events of the story so far, finishing with: "And you were all on the verandah, and you were looking at Namsti ..."

"Nam–as–te," Freddie said with a laugh.

"Yeah! Sorry. Nam–as–te. Go on. What happened next?"

Freddie smiled, drew his breath, looked into the distance and began again, quite slowly at first, as if he needed to warm up.

"After rescuing the little girl in the pink cardigan, I thought I had done what I'd been sent to do. I just didn't know. No one was telling me anything. I had to try and work it all out myself. And I was thinking how could I get back home? But the truth is, Connor, I wanted to stay because, I know it sounds mad, I didn't want to leave Namaste – not now I'd actually met her properly." He laughed nervously, unsure of his friend's reaction to this admission.

Connor smiled back and Freddie continued, reassured, "And if the journey back was going to be anything like as rough as getting there ..." he tailed off.

When it was suddenly realised that Freddie had no shoes on, the brother of the girl in the pink cardigan was sent from the crowded Namche verandah on a search. Thinking they had been lost in the rescue, the small boy scoured the ground nearby. Freddie felt bad about him going off on a wild goose chase, but he could hardly explain the truth to them.

Eventually Namaste was dispatched somewhere by her father. Freddie's eyes followed her down the now busy again street, until she was lost in the crowd.

A cheerful man appeared from the house opposite with some hot sweet tea and biscuity cake pieces. Freddie ate four in quick succession and felt much better.

Namaste returned, almost dragging an old lady who had a permanent grin on her wonderfully lined face. She took hold of Freddie's feet, quite roughly he thought, for someone who looked so nice. He winced as she sized them up, realising he had many more small cuts than he had first thought. She chuckled, said something that made everyone laugh, then disappeared.

Rather embarrassingly, Namaste's mother washed Freddie's feet and tended to the cuts and grazes. She even rubbed in some strong-smelling cream, which stung agonisingly, but Freddie put on a brave face in front of a certain onlooker. Five minutes later, the old lady returned with two pristine shoe boxes. She proudly presented their contents – two pairs of wonderful leather walking boots, which she gestured for him to try on. There was a new pair of thick hiking socks too, which Freddie gratefully pulled onto his feet.

As he held the second sock ready to put on, he caught Namaste's eye and gave it a small wave in her direction. She burst out laughing and had to hold her hand over her mouth to contain her giggles.

The first boots wouldn't fit over the socks, but the second pair were perfect in every way. Eager hands tugged at the laces and soon Freddie was the proud owner of the most magnificent brown leather climbing boots in Nepal.

His hands shot to his pockets, remembering the coins. He offered them in an attempted to pay, but he was assured they were a reward for his valiant efforts. The message came in stereo, in sign language from the very old man, and in glorious, halting English from Namaste.

"For you please, to take ... no money, for is pleasant. No! *prez–zant!*"

Freddie bowed his thanks and helped escort Namaste's father off the verandah. He said something in reply to a question from his daughter and gesticulated grandly to the streets and the hills. She turned, smiled, and said, "My father says, if you like ... to thank you, I can show you our Namche Bazaar."

"Thank *me*. No, no. Thank *you*! I'd really like that. Please," Freddie said, rubbing his hands nervously over the pockets filled with his old socks. He thought he ought to find a bin pretty quickly, or they might start attracting flies.

"My name is Mindhu," she bowed, with her hands in the prayer position.

"Oh! Is it?" Freddie almost sounded disappointed. "I mean, good. What a lovely name. Sorry, I thought you were called something else. I mean, my name is Freddie," he said, feeling the red glow rising in his cheeks once again. "Freddie Malone."

Embarrassment was replaced by the thrilling thought of spending time alone with Mindhu.

She stood patiently in the street waiting for him to descend the steps. At first Freddie felt like a deep-sea diver walking along the ocean floor, but the boots were really comfortable, rising above his ankle and giving him a fantastic feeling of support. They began walking down the road together.

"How do you know English so well?" Freddie asked.

"Everyone here does learnt, *no*! – does learns it in school," she replied. "It is the language of our visitors. Many travellers come. Namche is the best place to get by Everest from Nepal. This is very 'portant place."

"Wow. Everest," Freddie said in wonder. Mindhu nodded.

"You call her Everest. To us she is Sagarmatha or Chomolangma, 'The Mother Goddess of the sky'. We love her, and fear her ... and we pray to her." It was the first time Freddie had ever heard someone call a mountain 'her'. He was used to ships being referred to like this, but it gave Everest a new dimension. Not a huge dangerous rock, but a living entity, with moods, passions and feelings.

Mindhu changed the subject. "I had to leave school, because my parents now is ... err, now *are* too old and sick. I take my family's yaks up from Namche. Go up high to Thyangboche, to Gorak Shep and on to the Khumbhu glacier. We go all the way to Everest Base Camp. It is taking one day to Thyangboche ... where the monastery is very beautiful."

"Oh right. Is that the palace I saw over there?" Freddie gesticulated in the approximate direction.

"Yes, I'm sure that's what you saw."

"With Saga ... Sag ... err ... Everest behind it?"

"Yes. She stands behind Thyangboche, but many miles, many days away."

"Wow," said Freddie, feeling a little short of superlatives.

"Wow," said Mindhu, smiling and copying her companion. "From Thyangboche we travel high, through Pangboche, Pheriche, Dugla, and in one, two ... *three* days we find Gorak Shep. Then we move to Base Camp. It lasts four days for me, but you must take eight – nine days, not less."

"And bingo, that's all there is to it!" Freddie blurted.

"Been go? What this means?"

"Ah! It means, Err ... bingo! You've done it. Bingo!"

"Bingo – good. Yes, bingo then."

Freddie nodded and felt ridiculous. Why was he talking about Bingo?

Unaware of how irrelevant her latest English lesson had been, Mindhu continued, "You must clima ... Acc–limatise. Air is very thin."

At that moment they emerged from the shop-cluttered street into the market square, a hundred or so metres from the cliff edge.

Freddie could not ever remember being this happy. They stepped from the shade of the street to the brightness of the bustling bazaar. The heady mixture of the altitude, the location and recent events, mixed with the thick smoke rising from the fires, the fluttering of ten thousand coloured prayer flags, and the gorgeous girl at his side, made him feel like a king.

A king indeed. The King of Namche Bazaar!

Chapter Eight

Connor laughed at the King of Namche Bazaar, who was now sitting on a humble park bench, rather than a throne. Freddie opened his rucksack and lifted out a large pack of sandwiches wrapped in kitchen foil. Underneath, Connor could see a bulging blue and white striped plastic carrier bag, and next to that, the mysterious box with G.L.M. clearly showing on the lid.

What on earth was in it?

Freddie told him about the market in Namche as he offered Connor first choice of the sandwiches.

"It was amazing, Connor – no stalls, or tables, or any real order. Just long, rough rows on the ground, like a huge jumble sale, or a car boot sale – except without the cars, or the car boots!"

"These traders ... is Tibetans," Mindhu told him. "They

trek here long days, over high mountain passes. They have better chance to sell, in Namche. They carry ... from their villages in Tibet. It's big long walk for days, 'cross high, cold places, to trade for few nice–ties."

"Nice ties!" exclaimed Freddie. "Nice–ti ... Oh, you mean *necessities*, Mindhu. It's ne–cess–it–ies."

"Yes ... nice–*issi*–ties. Is that right?"

"Perfect." Freddie beamed.

"Then they carry ... all way back 'cross mountains to sell in Tibet. Back and froth – back and froth. Lan-slides – earthkrakes, still they walk."

Just then a new group of traders arrived. Freddie thought they looked completely shattered. They slowly set out their things, glancing nervously around at other people's stock. They were stuck in the shade, on the end of the furthest row, so their goods hardly looked enticing. Freddie dawdled as long as possible by their scant offerings, spread out on plastic sheets. It was rubbish really; rags, dirty old jumpers and hats that all looked like they had been worn by twenty people already. There were half packets of candles and razor blades and even some used soap. But they did have shoes, so Freddie's instincts about what he thought he could find at the bazaar had been right.

Whilst Freddie and Mindhu browsed, a boy picked up a pair of old trainers from the Tibetan's dismal collection, inspected them and then held them against his own feet. Some stern bartering took place and eventually he paid for them with three coins and his own flip-flops in part exchange. The flip flops were inspected by the Tibetans, brushed, washed, wiped, dried, and put in pride of place at the front of the display. Still warm, no doubt.

Mindhu knew the boy and they joked with each other before he scampered off. He was called Saylor and was excited because he had just got a good job as a porter on an expedition to Everest Base Camp, one which Mindhu and her yaks would do some work on as well. Saylor was to be employed by the group for the next six weeks, to go backwards and forwards with supplies, messages and equipment, whilst the American climbers set up camps for a summit attempt later in the year. As was customary, Saylor had been given an advance payment to get new clothes for himself and his first stop had been the footwear department of the newly arrived Tibetans. Mindhu translated his parting words. "End of the row, in the shade, means the lowest price."

They caught sight of Saylor twice more. Each time he was sporting further new layers of old clothes. He had virtually changed shape and looked very pleased.

Freddie and Mindhu now stood on the edge of the market by the *stupa*.

"Stupa is shrine, Mr Freddie," Mindhu explained helpfully. Next to them was the cliff face falling three thousand feet away down to a raging river-filled canyon.

You wouldn't want to be a sleep walker in this town.

Mindhu was very proud of Namche and told Freddie about the colourful prayer flags, or *darchok*, that hung everywhere and the ornate prayer wheels, which people turned as they passed. She pointed to the mouth-watering burgers that were drying on every available rock, but before she could explain, Freddie asked, "Do they taste good?"

He thought Mindhu might explode with laughter. Once she calmed down she explained that the 'burgers' were in fact patties of yak dung drying in the sun, which were used as fuel on fires all over the Himalayas. It stopped them having to chop down trees for firewood and it also explained the extremely strong smell of the smoke from the fires around the town.

Freddie was suitably embarrassed, but he knew it was a pretty funny thing to have got wrong. Just to set Mindhu off again, he picked up a yak-dung burger and pretended to eat it, whilst happily rubbing his stomach. She roared again. Freddie wished he had chosen a slightly drier one to mess around with and secretly checked if his hand smelt when Mindhu wasn't looking. He wiped it on the socks still hidden in his pocket.

To illustrate the scene, Freddie held up his hand to Connor, which contained the last uneaten sandwich. Completely engrossed, Connor had finished two and a half rounds of cheese and pickle. Freddie looked down at the empty foil on the bench, smiled and shook his head in amusement. Then, without a word, he took a modest bite from his half and handed over the rest.

"Your need is greater than mine," he added.

Connor finished the sandwich rather sheepishly and screwed up the foil to put back in the rucksack. Freddie saw him looking at the box in the bottom of the bag.

"All in good time, Connor," he said calmly.

It was a Saturday, so the park was quite busy. Was that Kelvin standing in the queue by the distant ice cream van, Connor wondered?

Freddie said, "Where were we?"

"Yak-dung burgers!" came the helpful reply, through a mouthful of sandwich.

He and Mindhu went to a cafe owned by her cousin, Tara, a dapper man in a huge apron. It had a few tables and chairs outside and overlooked the entire square. From where Freddie sat in the warm afternoon sunshine, he had a clear view up the main street. Tara gave them a huge pot of steaming hot chocolate and two large wedges of a dense dark cake.

Just then, two large, scruffy, bearded men invaded the terrace, in much the same way that they had barged through the game of marbles earlier. They sat down at the table next to Freddie, blocking most of the view and all the warming rays of the sun. One was blonde and surly looking. The darker, larger man ordered Tara about like a dog and smoked a huge, smelly cigar. He blew the fumes everywhere, and already the café's other customers were looking at him with increasing distaste. Freddie thought he had a grim mask of a face which fitted the way he behaved.

The breeze caught the clouds of smoke and drove them continually towards the back of Mindhu's head. Freddie could not bear to think of the vile smell coating her shiny, long black hair. She didn't seem to notice as she talked about her family.

Mindhu had one brother left at home, Passang, who was older than her. Her other surviving brothers and sisters no longer helped with the business and lived in Kathmandu. She looked suddenly at the floor and Freddie thought the cigar smoke was finally upsetting her, but it wasn't that. When he asked what was wrong, Mindhu whispered the tragic tale of her favourite brother, Binoi, who was killed by an avalanche in the Khumbu Icefall, on Everest.

"He was going to climb Sagarmatha, Everest, to the top," she said, with moist eyes. "He never did …er … making it. One day, I will climb for him …"

Freddie heard her voice waver. He wanted to give her a massive hug, but settled instead for changing the subject. Mindhu looked at him gratefully, and after a while her smile returned.

In Nepalese terms her family were wealthy, as a herd of yaks and a thriving relay business ensured great standing in the community. However, it was too much work for her and Passang, both of whom had left school earlier than they wanted.

"Otherwise my English would be more ... more better," Mindhu apologised.

"It's perfect, and it's a lot better than my Nepali. All I can say is 'Namaste'."

"But you say it very well, Mr Freddie," Mindhu beamed.

"Thank you. Does Namaste mean 'hello'?"

"It means that, yes. It also means 'How are you?', and 'Good day' and 'What a view!' and 'Isn't it hot?' and 'My legs hurt' – all things like that."

"I wish we had a word as useful as that," he laughed and then coughed as a result of the growing fug from the cigar.

He talked about the Everest project they had done at school, but was careful not to mention anything about the date back at home, as he was still trying to find out what year it was in Nepal.

"Where I live everyone is fascinated by Ever ... *Sagar–matha*."

She smiled every time he corrected himself and gently touched his sleeve as if to say it was perfectly acceptable to say Everest. As she did so, a shot of electricity surged through his arm and he pulled it away, nearly knocking over the pot of hot chocolate. Mindhu looked worried that she might have offended Freddie by touching him, but he eventually managed to convince her that it was his fault and she had taken him by surprise, that was all.

It was Freddie's turn to put a reassuring hand on her arm. She looked up and as their eyes met, a feeling of warmth swept over them both. Slightly embarrassed to be seen like this, if they *could* be seen through the thick cigar smoke, Mindhu pretended to pull her arm away as if struck by an electric shock, just as Freddie had done. They smiled at the shared joke and although the moment was broken, the warm feeling wasn't lost. Freddie felt elated as he sat and stared in awe at this perfect girl. He didn't think that Phoebe or Chloe or any of the girls at school had ever had quite this effect.

"Who is – *are*, you here with? They will be missing you? It is late."

Freddie gulped like a cartoon character, then coughed again, giving himself more time to invent an answer. He sifted through the half-constructed collection of white lies in his head, trying to find a reply to this impossible question.

He took a big breath, fixed Mindhu with what he hoped looked like an honest expression and said confidently, "Well ..."

He was cut short by the angry voice of Mr Cigar Breath, who was insulting an elderly American trekker who had dared complain about the foul smoke.

"If you don't like it, go and find another mountain to climb. This one's ours, and we like cigars, so get lost."

The couple immediately left the café, clearly frightened by the huge, uncouth man. He scowled at the remaining clientele, who quickly turned their heads to avoid a similar confrontation. Only Freddie held the man's gaze as his cruel eyes panned around, but he was instantly dismissed as just a boy – no threat at all. Freddie thought he would remember the man and his awful behaviour for a long time. One thing was certain, he would remember the smell of the cigar forever.

It was even worse that the thug appeared to be British, although he had a slightly mixed up sort of Englishy–American accent. Eventually, the two brutish men finished their drinks and left in a swirl of smoke, leaving the remaining customers to relax again and return to their conversations.

"Where was I?" asked Freddie.

"Your friends, they will be worried," repeated Mindhu.

Freddie, still no closer to an answer, gulped.

Chapter Nine

"Yeah! Right! Yes. I really should be getting back to, er, the rest of my group," Freddie stuttered. "Further up, y'know, just past … where I met you. I only came to Namche to get some new boots as my other shoes kept … slipping." The second lie left his mouth before he could stop it.

Mindhu looked upset and Freddie thought it was because she knew he was lying, but he soon realised that was impossible. Only someone who had arrived through a time-tunnel-vortex-type-transporter thingummy, would have any need to disguise the truth.

"You must go before it gets dark," she offered sadly.

The realisation that he must leave Mindhu and somehow return home hit Freddie hard. The sun left the small terrace and an unwelcome chill instantly hit the pair of them.

They dawdled back up the street and Mindhu told

Freddie he had less than two hours of daylight left. If he ran out of time and wasn't going to reach his friends, he must stop climbing and descend immediately back to Namche.

"You must come to my home," she said, smiling and pointing to a larger than average house with a big paddock spreading up behind it, containing the now peacefully grazing yaks. He looked longingly at the house, wishing he didn't have to leave her. But how else could he explain his presence here other than lie?

Just before they parted, Freddie put a question to Mindhu.

"So, Mindhu, I've been thinking, you're a Buddhist – right?'"

"Yes Freddie Malone, I is. No! I *am*." She beamed a smile.

"I was wondering, in Buddhism, err ... do you have the same calendar? You know, I mean years and months, type of thing, like we do in England? Because some religions have different dates and ... things," he stammered, his inspiration once again running thin. Mindhu interrupted his ramblings with a rapturous smile.

"Yes Mr Freddie Malone, you have to believe, it is 1989 in Nepal too. Poor little backwards Nepal. We are still allowed to share the same date as you, Mr Freddie. We are also January 1989, as well as in your big England. In fact Mr Big Man Freddie, we are well ahead of you. I learn in school, the sun rises in Nepal long time before it rises in your big England, Mr Freddie. So we are really ahead of you silly people." She treated him to her most hypnotic laugh.

Freddie laughed too, not only because he had found out *when* he was here, but because Mindhu was the funniest girl he had ever met.

She told him to get going before it was too late, adding that she hoped she would meet him again further up the mountain, as she was leaving for Sagarmatha in the morning with a full yak train. Freddie promised he would look out for her and as she began singing again, she disappeared from view.

Now he had some very hard work to do before he got to the shelter of the hut he had seen earlier. The climb was tough on Freddie, but his new boots made things so much easier. Some porters overtook him, among them was Saylor, who was carrying a huge load, perfectly crowned by a toilet seat welded onto a set of metal chair legs.

"Namaste, Saylor," Freddie said. The shocked porter nearly lost his cargo, but beamed back an encouraging smile and continued his speedy ascent.

The light was dwindling and the temperature had already plummeted. Freddie revelled in the scenery, and his situation. He realised of course, it was all down to one thing; he had met a certain yak-train driver.

As is usually the way when you feel really good

about things, fate has a strange habit of turning round and smacking you in the teeth.

"I just couldn't believe my eyes when I staggered round the last bend before the hut," Freddie told Connor. "I was gutted. It was surrounded by porters, putting up tents and starting fires, and boiling water. All around the hut. And it was the only shelter for miles."

Just then, Freddie suddenly stopped telling Connor his story and looked nervously down at the ground, seemingly preoccupied by another thought.

Shouts and laughter, ball games, picnics and couples now spread out across the grass of the park. Freddie looked around and shifted his rucksack closer, opening the zip. He pulled out a couple of bananas, as if talking about the climb had made him hungry. He ate quickly in silence and seemed to be concentrating on something.

Two park wardens, one large and the other slight had begun to patrol their kingdom. Connor watched the contrasting figures strolling along and waited for Freddie to continue.

He seemed rather fidgety, fiddling with the bag and rearranging things. The park wardens walked behind them and started shouting at someone behind the shrubs. "Get outta there. Come on, scarper! There's plenty of space in the park." Then they carried on along the long path.

"What did you do then? Where did you go?" Connor asked.

Freddie picked up the discarded banana peel, stuffed it in the carrier bag and put it in a bin a few metres past the next bench. He turned back, smiling.

Freddie was about to say something, when suddenly four screaming figures erupted from the bushes. It was Jasper, Maz, Rowan and Paul. Freddie and Connor were now separated by a distance of ten metres, with Jasper's gang closing on them fast. Connor scrambled up from the bench and started to run in the direction of the pond where there was the promise of safety in numbers. Freddie saw the line Connor was taking and managed to deliver a breathless message out of the corner of his mouth as they passed each other.

"Get to the oak!"

Freddie veered away. Connor kept running with his head bent, waiting for a smack on the back, or a rugby tackle which would bring him down in the mud and glass of the empty pond. But nothing happened. Freddie peeled away to the right, giving the pursuers two trails to follow and splitting their manpower.

It was not until Connor was at the far side of the

park, miraculously still in one piece, that he looked back. He lingered near the park wardens, who were now removing graffiti from a sign. They gave him a funny look as he caught his breath, hands on knees, purple-faced and shoulders heaving with effort. Connor still expected a punch at any second. But nothing came. He scanned the park for Freddie. He saw with relief that his friend must have escaped, because now their attackers were regrouping around the bench.

To Connor's amazement, sitting and swinging his little legs (not even long enough to touch the path), was Kelvin. He had a massive smile on his face, shouting and waving at Jasper – proudly displaying the captured rucksack.

Freddie's rucksack.

The bag that contained the mysterious and precious tin box.

Jasper ripped it away from Kelvin and waved it in the direction Freddie had taken. They all started jumping up and down in celebration, parading the stolen bounty above their heads like marauding pirates. Kelvin couldn't reach up to the bag however hard he tried. It was obvious he had given Freddie's and Connor's location away to get in with the gang, but he was still the odd one out. Connor was sure Kelvin had been used. And come to think of it, so in turn had he, by Kelvin. Connor hung his head and felt totally gutted. His big mouth had ruined everything. Why had he told Kelvin about the tin? He closed his eyes and cursed himself. *You idiot! You total idiot.*

Kelvin was still jumping up, trying to reach the bag, when he was suddenly rounded on by the other four; like a pack of hyenas turning on the weakest. Kelvin soaked up some half-hearted slaps from the group.

One of the wardens, the large one with the big paunch and moustache, stopped wiping the sign and turned to Connor.

"What's up, young un? You alright?" he asked.

Connor gasped, catching his breath. "Thanks … Yes … It's just a game … They've stolen my mate's rucksack … But we'll get it back." He walked away quickly, smiling as best he could. This was now anything but a game.

Connor marched along the busy road, checking every fifty metres to make sure he wasn't being followed. Once he was sure he was on his own, he began to make his way to the woods, taking the busiest streets to try and avoid further attack from the new owners of the rucksack.

Connor ran through his counter-surveillance moves. He was proud of his abilities, practised with Freddie over the previous two holidays and helped by reading bits of books by an old man who used to be in the SAS. Connor's elder brother, Carl, was always reading stuff like that and talking about it with their dad. It was about as excited as the pair of them ever got.

The plan started with a simple corner turn, taking the first turning right. As soon as he was out of sight, he planned to disappear behind a hedge or wall. That way he could spot his enemy approaching. Then, once they'd passed, he could move in the opposite direction and get back to the main road. But Connor hadn't accounted for the large number of people taking advantage of a warm August Saturday, mowing lawns and trimming hedges. There was no obvious place to hide, so he had no option other than to slope back to the main road.

Never mind, he thought. *Try again*.

Next, he adopted the ever reliable 'drop-and-turn manoeuvre'. You drop something onto the pavement, stoop down, turn and look back, all in one slick move. It was meant to be executed quickly to take the enemy completely by surprise. Connor searched his pockets for an object to discard. The only thing he had was a £5 note. Just as he let it drop, a breeze caught it and took it in a series of hops under a parked car. By the time he eventually retrieved the dirty note, it was too late to spot if anyone was following him.

Humiliated, Connor stopped by a newsagents, pretending to read the adverts in the window and occasionally flicking his eyes back down the road. In between reading about people who would be thrilled to do his ironing, or dig his garden, or babysit for him, he surveyed everyone who looked in the least bit suspicious. But there was no sign of a vicious gang brandishing a green and silver rucksack.

Connor went into the shop, remembering that the old SAS man had said, "Always eat, drink, and stock up while you have the chance."

Great advice, Connor thought as he surveyed, wide-eyed, the pristine ranks of chocolate bars and sweets.

What would the SAS pick for this mission? he wondered, licking his lips.

Chapter Ten

Connor was now deep in Jasper country, on the corner of Travers Road, trying to plan the safest route to the oak. Suddenly, he heard excited laughter and four familiar voices all battling to talk at once. If they spotted him, he was sunk. There was no way he could outrun them with a start of only a hundred metres. He needed more like a kilometre.

As Connor peered out from behind the post box, he could see Jasper proudly wearing the rucksack, as the others danced in attendance around him.

"Did you see their faces?" crowed Maz.

"They'll have run home to their mummies," Rowan added.

Then Jasper did an exaggerated impersonation of Connor, running away wearing the rucksack on his front pretending it was a huge stomach, shuffling like an inflated penguin.

"Look! This was Fat Boy," he shouted.

Connor wanted to yell, "I don't run like that, idiot!" But he bit his lip.

They all did an impression in turn, each one magnifying the imitation. They waddled about, bumping into each other and shouting in silly, high-pitched voices.

Connor couldn't do anything but stare at them. Was this how everybody saw him? He had visions of his parents joining in, bouncing round their lounge during the ad breaks. A bald man emerged from his side gate and gestured to them.

"Take your racket somewhere else."

The gang were shocked into silence for a second, but then Jasper shouted, "Slaphead!" at him and made a few rude gestures.

The shocked man retreated to the sanctuary of his high-walled garden and the gang sauntered away. To Connor's great relief, they continued away from him along Offord Road.

Should he continue on to the woods, or follow them? Should he get to the Oak, or keep tabs on the rucksack and its precious contents?

His eye was suddenly drawn to a figure moving on the opposite pavement, slinking along in the shadow of a fence fifty metres away. It was Kelvin.

Suddenly, a hand grabbed Connor's chin and

another gripped the back of his head. He tried to scream and bite the hand that covered his mouth. Then he scraped his heel down the front of his attacker's legs. His elbow made contact with the side of a head, but then his arms were pulled back sharply. Jasper must have gone round the block and attacked him from behind. They struggled on and just as Connor was tiring, a voice whispered frantically in his ear, "Stop it, Connor! It's me! It's Freddie!"

Connor didn't know whether to laugh or cry. What made it all the more funny was that Freddie was hopping about in agony where his shins had been raked, whilst shaking his bitten hand. He looked like a drunk Morris dancer, yelping and trying desperately not to alert Kelvin.

Thankfully, Freddie looked like he was starting to see the funny side. He rubbed the side of his head and whispered to Connor, "With friends like you, who needs enemies?"

"Sorry."

"You've done more damage to me in fifteen seconds than Jasper's managed in two years. You don't know your own strength," he whispered with a smile.

"Why didn't you text me?" Connor asked.

"Because my phone's in the rucksack!"

They watched Kelvin stalking Jasper, then

each recounted their movements since leaving the park. Freddie's experience had been very similar to Connor's, except Freddie had been able to run a lot further and a lot faster, and hadn't had his anti surveillance techniques shown up as rubbish. Once he was out of sight, he had immediately doubled back to the park, and followed Kelvin on parallel roads.

"What about the secret box?" Connor asked.

"The box?"

"Yes!"

"It's still in the park."

"What?"

Freddie nodded.

"I heard stuff going on in the bushes behind us, whispers and rustling, while I was talking to you. So I put the tin in the carrier bag with the ... with the other thing I brought back from Nepal, as well as our rubbish, so it would all look like junk. Then I took it to the bin so it wouldn't fall into enemy hands. I thought I could get it once Jasper left the park, then they ganged up on Kelvin."

Hang on, Connor thought. He must have missed something. "What's this other ..."

Freddie cut in quickly. "I watched from the same bushes from where they'd burst out and attacked us. They soon got bored and ran off. They left Kelvin there blubbing. I was about to get the box, when the park wardens came and emptied the bins and put new bags in."

"No!"

"Yes!" Freddie continued. "So I waited until Kelvin dragged himself away and then followed the wardens with the bin bags to the dump behind their shed, y'know – at the bottom end of the park. They threw them into a massive pile of bags and our bag went somewhere against the far mesh wall, right in line with a metal post that sticks out at the top."

"How do you know it's there?"

"Well, there were only a few bags and they threw them up to the top of the pile. I watched really closely. All the bags went in the same place. I'm positive they all ended up against the wall. Then I got spotted and the big one with the 'tache shouted at me. I didn't know what to do. He wasn't really, like, angry, but he was asking me what I wanted, and I couldn't think of an excuse. My brain just wasn't working. One minute I was telling you about Nepal and hot chocolate and then ... I thought if I asked him to open the bags, he'd steal what was inside. It's just too valuable Connor. I still can't think straight." Freddie sighed. "But I knew if I found you, you'd think of something. So, what shall we do?"

Connor puffed out his chest and thought hard, feeling very flattered to be asked.

"Right. Let's get to the Oak and you can finish telling me about Namche and the box. Then, when the park closes, I'll climb over the fence and go through the bags while you keep watch and I'll get your special box, y'know ... and this other, whatever thingy."

He trailed off, hoping Freddie would fill in the blanks for him, but no such luck. A little smile danced on Freddie's blotchy face.

"All in good time, Connor. But that's a good plan. I knew you'd think of something. Let's disappear and wait for Jasper to lose interest."

Ten minutes later they found the abandoned rucksack squashed into a bin near Jasper's house. There was no sign of Freddie's phone though.

"Oh no! My mum will go berserk," Freddie said. "I only got it on Sunday."

The bag was dusty, dirty and totally empty, a bit like how Connor and Freddie both felt.

They perched in the branches of the huge old oak tree, with its great views of all the approaching paths. Freddie got himself comfortable, dangling his legs either side of a big bough, worn smooth by generations of hiding boys. He planted his back firmly against the thick trunk, drew a breath, and in an instant they were back in the magical kingdom of the fluttering prayer flags.

Freddie was devastated to see the hut surrounded by the porters. He was spotted by Saylor, who waved urgently and jabbered rapidly in his eccentric English.

"Dane juice. *Dane—juice*," Saylor said. Freddie was mystified.

"Dane juice?" Freddie repeated, turning the words over in his head. He helped Saylor attached an orange sheet to four upright poles that were hammered into the frozen ground.

Saylor play-acted being dead and said, "*Dane* juice."

This time it made sense to Freddie.

"Ah! Dangerous! Dan—*ger*—ous. I understand."

"Yes. Dane—*err*—juice," said Saylor, with a triumphant smile. Eventually, it was established that Saylor thought it would be mad to go further tonight and Freddie was welcome to share their camp. Freddie gratefully accepted, and when the makeshift loo stood as strong and inviting as it was ever going to get, Freddie was introduced to each man in turn.

First of all, there was Lally, who spoke enough good English to communicate easily. He was quite large in comparison to many Nepali men and was dressed in high quality mountain kit. This was because he was the boss, known as a *sirdar*.

"I Lally. I in charge of porter supplies ... and the safe carry, evvy—thing up down mountain. This my house," he said with a broad and proud smile.

He was introduced to the cook, Ghito, a tiny man

with bandy legs and an air of importance. Although smaller than most of the others, he rattled orders nearly as loudly as the pots that he crashed about.

Then came Mingma, who was older than Saylor – maybe twenty or so, but taller and leaner. His smile was more difficult to ignite. He told Freddie, "My fambly from Langtang Valley – very poor. One day, I desire is to be famous Sherpa. I is study an' train hard, to getting my dream." Mingma was keen to practise his English. "I … err, I want to climbing Sagarmatha … in the footsteps of my hero … Sherpa Tensing Norgay."

Freddie hoped Mingma would fulfil his dream.

Twenty or so introductions followed, but the final porter would not be an easy boy to forget. He was about Freddie's age, willowy and fit, with a floppy quiff of jet black hair which lollopped onto his forehead. He was simply known as 'Elvis'. It was perfect. He had been given the nickname by an American climber years before and the name had stuck.

Everyone except Lally was dressed in motley hand-me-down clothes and shoes. The Tibetan department store at Namche had certainly been busy today.

So Lally, Ghito, Saylor, Mingma, Elvis and Freddie whiled away the ferociously cold evening doing jobs. It was a good feeling to earn his keep, and Freddie counted out plates and provisions with Lally for the evening meal.

Next, he assisted Ghito to cook *dal bhat* and a dish

called *tarkari*, adding a "magic mix–it–ture" (as Ghito called it) – his garam masala, a mouth-watering blend of pungent spices, increasing the wonderful smell of the lentil curry. Freddie felt faint with hunger.

Freddie turned to Connor and said, "What a day! If it had all ended then, I would still have had the best day of my life. I still had no idea what I was doing there, or how I was going to get back, but you know something? I realised I just wanted to stay in Nepal – stay in the mountains. I just wanted it to last forever."

"Yeah? Tell me about this curry," Connor drooled.

Chapter Eleven

Freddie hadn't eaten properly for hours, but he quickly made up for it. Eventually he sat back feeling happy and full and Saylor passed Freddie a flask.

"This is our home beer we make, called *chang*. Very strong. It help our people sleep, on cold nights," Saylor rolled his eyes. Freddie was not at all surprised it knocked people out because when he smelt it, his eyes watered instantly. It was like sticking a petrol pump up your nose. He had a sip, but thought any more might make him spend all night in the dreaded toilet tent.

The moon rose from behind the beautiful pointed summit of Ama Dhablam. The chang circulated, and a round-faced porter with a cheeky grin cried, "Cheers!" Soon everyone was saying it and toasting Freddie's earlier heroics. It was decided that he should sleep in Lally's hut, being the only shelter available fit for a hero.

He was kitted out with spares from the expedition's

equipment by the smiling Elvis, who handed over a sleeping bag and a navy blue goose-down jacket. A logo on the chest read: 'Climbing Kings. Everest. 1989. Watch us Go.'

"You save young grill's life – so we help you, best we able," Elvis said.

"Namaste," said Freddie.

The interior of the shelter was very basic, but pride of place went to a small, rotund, smiling Buddha on a simple shrine, surrounded by plastic flowers. In the opposite corner, a battered mattress lay on a solid low platform. Lally created an elaborate lair for himself on the floor using some yak furs and Freddie slept top to toe with Saylor on the bed, swamped in his goose -down sleeping bag, which was more than a match for the cold at that altitude.

Saylor told him, "Tempy–ratcher last night five degrees, minus. But tomorrow, it be ten degrees minus at Thyangboche."

There was the slightly off-putting smell of Saylor's feet, just inches from his nose, but he managed to blot it out by rolling over and thinking about the wonderful curry.

Morning found him refreshed. All around Lally's hut there was a quiet but spectacularly fast packing process going on. Freddie returned his jacket and sleeping bag to Elvis, who instead offered him a small daysack to stow the two articles in. He could see several porters already on the move up the path.

"Thyangboche Mon—is—attery." Elvis told him. "Very hard day. Long climbing ahead."

Freddie reassured Lally he would meet up with his missing friends at the monastery and was it alright if he tagged along for the day? Lally made Freddie feel like it was an honour he was joining them.

Saylor said, "It will be lunchtime before we saw, err, we see Mindhu and yaks. Which your favo'rit yak Freddie? Which one you waitin' to see!" He and Elvis giggled. Freddie smiled awkwardly. Was it that obvious he liked Mindhu?

A glorious morning followed, with views ahead to Thyangboche, and before they started the ferocious descent down to Thamserku, the far distant wonders of Nuptse, Lhotse, and Everest, with the beautiful Ama Dhablam always on their right. It was a never-ending series of hairpin switchbacks as the line of porters kicked up dust from the dry path. Freddie could see why Saylor didn't want the yaks too close behind them on this section. Mingma lent Freddie a blue cotton scarf to tie round his nose to stop too much of the dust getting in.

It was late morning by the time they stopped in a small paddock by a sharp bend in the river. Everyone peeled off boots and socks or, in some cases, plimsolls, to tend to their feet. The cheeky porter yelped with mock pain as he dipped his toes into the freezing meltwater.

Freddie had a good wash and examined his new boots for wear and tear. It was whilst he sat propped up against the dry stone wall that he heard the first clatter of bells, found in this part of the world only on the collars of yaks.

Mindhu was loosening a scarf from her face as she came round the corner. Her eyes met Freddie's. He stood and waved, followed by a dusty, "Namaste."

This time his 'Namaste' was different again. It meant 'Hello. I've missed you. I've been thinking of nothing else since I saw you last. I worship the ground you and your yaks walk on ... and, oh no! I've got my socks in my hand again.'

Mindhu gushed a joyous peel of laughter and a blushing Freddie dusted off his feet and quickly replaced his socks and boots. Then Mindhu was again by his side, having led the yaks to a paddock. She gave a small bow and he noticed that today she was dressed in a much smarter grey top and black trousers. She looked amazing.

"Namaste, Freddie, No! sorry ... Mr! Yes please. Mr Freddie Malone, I am very pleased to see you again, so soon."

"Me too, yes. I'm ... Hello, Mindhu. Not as pleased as I am."

It all came out wrong, but she smiled and invited him to help tend the yaks with her brother. Freddie was introduced to Passang. He nodded back politely. There was a definite family likeness, although Passang's natural expression was slightly sad.

Freddie threw himself into a whirl of activity, trying to help, and maybe impress a little. Once or twice he caught Saylor and Elvis looking at him over the low wall that divided the paddocks. They wore slightly conspiratorial smiles, but Freddie didn't mind. He wasn't going to let Saylor and Elvis stop him from spending time with Mindhu, just to appear to be one of the lads.

Everyone prepared for the afternoon ahead. Mindhu walked to a tiny roadside shop with Freddie. She bought some soap and a comb, saying she had forgotten to bring hers. Once they emerged into the bright light, Mindhu pointed out some revolving prayer wheels. Those he had seen so far were turned by hand as you passed, offering up the carved prayers as the wheel spun. These bigger ones were driven just like mill wheels by the rushing water.

Then straps were tightened, fodder stowed and animals checked and prepared. Passang led the largest and most ferocious yak away first. With whoops of encouragement from Mindhu, the rest dutifully followed and the difficult two-thousand-foot climb to Thyangboche Monastery began. Freddie walked with Mindhu at the rear of the rumbling yak train. The pain and joy of the climb were linked so closely, they became one unforgettable experience. Uncle Patrick's words echoed constantly as he tried to keep up with her.

"It's the journey that's important, not the destination."

It made perfect sense.

He had included another of Uncle Patrick's sayings in his Everest project, and it had earned him an A grade: Take only photographs, leave only footprints. He shared them with Mindhu during one brief stop.

"They mean good things," she said smiling. "I understand."

The climb was not terribly sociable. The scarves were once more tied over noses and mouths and for the first hour the ascent felt almost vertical, back and forth on more dusty hairpins. This was replaced for the second hour by a long, straight, upward slog. Occasionally, Freddie did have to rest; such was his difficulty in breathing. Each time he stalled, Mindhu would turn, smile and encourage him.

Eventually the dusty path gave way to a stony one, and it was wonderful to drop the face mask. Mindhu was concentrating on her charges as the yak's hooves skittered on the shiny rock. Freddie was truly exhausted and nearly at the extremes of his endurance, but he summoned his remaining strength to keep up with her.

It was worth the effort. He crested a ridge, fully expecting to see another gruelling uphill section ahead.

Instead, spread before him, with the sun glinting off its windows, was the magnificent sight of Thyangboche Monastery. All he could do was stand and marvel at the ornate complex of courtyards and carvings, windows and balconies. And there, framed behind in bright sunlight, stood Everest and its mighty plume.

Freddie tried not to blink in case this magical moment was taken away from him. All around the monastery were monks and travellers in their brightly coloured robes and clothes.

Past Freddie, over the ridge, came the first of the weary column. It was the cheeky porter. He smiled and said, "Cheers."

Freddie couldn't think of anything funny to say in return and uttered simply, "Namaste." This time meaning 'I'm speechless!'

After helping to unload the yaks, Freddie told Mindhu that he had to look for his friends, and reluctantly dragged himself away, having arranged to meet her again when the monks blew the first horn for afternoon prayers. He didn't want to leave, but what else could he do? She would soon ask questions again that would be impossible for him to answer. Freddie needed to get his story sorted out.

In front of the monastery was a dusty flat area of bare earth about the size of two football pitches where a hundred tents of all shapes, colours and sizes were pitched. This was where the trekkers and mountaineers camped, some in measured and precise rows, others plonked on the first flat spot they came to.

Freddie knew he must find shelter for the night and was glad he still had the daysack with the down jacket and sleeping bag. Should he invent a story about his friends having lost his equipment? Or just continue to use them until someone asked for them back?

Walking slowly past a group of more elaborate tents, with a trekking tour company logo on the bright orange side panels, Freddie was amazed to see the large American lady who had trumpeted his heroics in Namche yesterday. He could only see her legs and bottom emerging backwards from a straining tent flap, but he knew it was her, alright! "I gotta getta picture of a lama," was all the clue he needed.

In the distance he could see some maroon-coloured figures kicking a weather-beaten ball about. As he approached, he was delighted to see they were young monks of about his own age.

Around the perimeter of the parade ground he saw little shacks, some basic shops, three tea houses, some wash houses and toilets. The latrines backed onto the huge drop that fell away from the plateau and seemed to balance precariously on the edge. It looked as if one strong gust could send them crashing the two thousand feet he had just staggered up.

The flurry of activity to complete crucial jobs

during the last minutes of daylight was in full swing. Freddie seemed to be the only person who witnessed the last rays of the sun touching Everest's peak. He wanted to point, and shout to everyone, "Stop! Look!" But gradually, even the highest point on Earth lost its spark. Freddie hoped he would still be around to see the first rays touch the summit tomorrow. Again, feelings of dread and anguish crammed his chest and head. The questions he kept asking himself were so unanswerable it made him dizzy.

Then some deep and thunderous notes sounded from huge horns announcing the call to prayer. He made his way to the gates of the monastery compound and joined people of all nationalities in the inner courtyard, and on to the large temple at its heart.

Suddenly, Mindhu was by his side and a surge of electricity jolted through his body. When Mindhu enquired politely how his friends were, Freddie stuttered a none too convincing reply about them all being tired and then hastily changed the subject.

Once inside the temple, Freddie observed Mindhu closely and copied her every move. People were taking off their shoes and boots and shuffling on across the cold flagstone floor. Freddie was mortified. What if his feet smelt really bad? Mindhu slipped off her battered training shoes and Freddie unlaced his boots. Luckily the care he had paid to his feet at lunchtime had paid off.

They sat close together in the magnificent temple and Freddie was lost in a totally new world.

He was high on a flat-topped mountain, in a far-off kingdom, surrounded by sights, sounds, smells and sensations that would be burnt into his memory forever.

By his side was Mindhu.

"All is well with the world, then," Uncle Patrick would have said.

Chapter Twelve

What followed was mesmerising. A constant bass 'parp' from huge droning horns, the tinkling of cymbals and random crashing of gongs combined with a sweet smell of incense and the hypnotic chanting of a hundred monks.

Mindhu and Freddie sat crossed-legged on the freezing stone floor. Freddie was very grateful that the down jacket was long enough to tuck under him.

Rows of maroon-robed monks of all ages filled the centre of the temple. Freddie's head and eyes darted back and forth, not wanting to miss a thing. Two tiny young monks, no older than ten, constantly circulated their elders with enormous tin teapots. They poured out steaming liquid, which was downed in grateful gulps.

On the dais, two teenage monks stood in attendance over a seated middle-aged, bald man in glasses.

Mindhu whispered, "Head Lama." The boys were in the middle of a fit of giggles. Maybe they had spotted the large American trekker opposite, still in her shorts, eyes closed, swaying to the hypnotic chants.

The proceedings were presided over by a huge, smiling, twenty-foot wooden statue of the Buddha, a much bigger brother of the one he had seen in Lally's hut.

In front of the dais was a large cabinet with glass panelled sides. Freddie supposed it held articles of religious significance. It was difficult to see exactly what they were from where he sat. The only thing he could definitely make out seemed to be an ancient-looking tin box bound by a leather strap. This occupied the bottom shelf, and above it, was what looked like the remnants of half a coconut. *It can't be a coconut though*, Freddie thought. *No religion would worship a coconut.* But that's what it looked like.

Then he realised he could see a perfect reflection of Mindhu in the glass of the cabinet, and what struck him after staring for some minutes was how neat her hair appeared. Freddie continued to gaze until a very old, wizened monk stood between him and the image of Mindhu. He was waving his hands about energetically. Freddie couldn't tell if he was keeping warm or performing a ritual.

Freddie was feeling braver now and his gaze swept round to the real Mindhu by his side. She had her eyes tightly closed and was mouthing the chants in time. Yes, she most certainly had combed her hair and there was just a trace of soap rising over the aroma of the incense. Freshly washed and brushed hair, with recently acquired comb and soap. Was it in his honour? Surely not. To think *that* would mean that Mindhu was ... and that she might *actually* ...

No! he cut himself off. Butterflies fluttered round his stomach. His mind was racing, trying not to get too excited about the evidence before him: Mindhu might actually *fancy* ...

Get real! he told himself again.

Her eyes flicked open and she caught him staring. But instead of saying, "Wot u lookin' at?" as Mia Bishop at school would say, Mindhu beamed a radiant smile at him. It said 'It's alright. I'm very glad you're looking at me.'

Then the realisation struck Freddie. He was from another time and another world. He might as well have been an alien visitor from Pluto. As wonderful as these moments were, they were just that: moments. Stolen moments. There was no future. In reality, he had not even been born yet. It was 1989 in Nepal. What would happen if he asked Mindhu to travel back to his time and his world? If indeed he could get back. These thoughts overwhelmed Freddie and by the time Mindhu looked at him again, there was a tear welling up in his eye that he was trying hard to ignore. He would explain to her later that the incense had got to him.

How Freddie would have loved to show Mindhu where he lived and meet his family, especially Uncle Patrick—

"And of course you, Connor," he added instantly.

But Mindhu would think he was completely mad if he started to try and explain what had happened to him.

The temple emptied and the only people left were the giggling attendants, who were busy extinguishing candles. As they stood and stretched their freezing limbs, Mindhu beckoned Freddie nearer to the cabinet to explain its contents.

"This was ... This *is* the very 'portant writings of Padma the ... Wives? No! I know ... *Wise*. Padma the Wise. This very 'portant. It has the secrets of all the whole world. Yes! You understand? His teacherings are writ' here, and will save world one day."

"They are beautiful Mindhu," Freddie stammered, not really having a clue what she was talking about.

Apart from the ornate parchment of Padma the Wise, which was decorated with the familiar swirling letters, there was an old tin box, in the middle of the bottom shelf. It had a worn leather strap pulled tight around it and the initials G.L.M. on the lid. All Mindhu knew about the rusty object was that it had belonged to a very brave mountaineer from England who had disappeared on the north face of Everest on the Tibetan side of the mountain.

"His body has never been found," she said sadly.

The small tin held his secrets, and had not been opened since it had been given to the monastery. No one knew for sure how long ago that was. The box was thought to contain the heroic mountaineer's spirit, and whilst it remained unopened, it acted as a burial for his lost soul. The Nepalese believed that if anyone opened the tin, the spirit of the brave climber would escape and be blown around the high mountains forever.

Freddie listened in awe to Mindhu, who seemed to know so much.

"I not know name of man who lives in box."

He shrugged as if to reassure Mindhu that she couldn't know everything about everything. Then a shiver coursed through him.

G.L.M.! The initials leapt out at him from the tin. Cogs in Freddie's brain began to turn.

Mindhu was telling Freddie about the manuscripts on the middle shelf and how important they were, as the two giggling monks continued to snuff out candles around them. Freddie's mind raced on, trying to solve the tin's riddle.

G.L.M. … *G.L.M.?*

What Mindhu said next, however, shocked him so completely that all else was forgotten. She pointed to what looked like the broken coconut shell, lying in two large pieces on the top shelf and she said quite calmly, "And this is the famous scalp of ... yeti."

She paused for dramatic effect, but she didn't really need to, Freddie was gawping open-mouthed at the rather hideous treasure. It was the size of it that got him. He swallowed hard and shook his head.

"Yeti! Wow! Is that ... err fur? Or bone? Is it? Or hair? No, I can't, err, wow!" Freddie stuttered.

Was it real? If this was the yeti's scalp, how big would it have made the beast itself? It would be at least ten feet tall, but he was only guessing. It could have been three feet tall with a massive head for all he knew.

Mindhu pointed to the dais where the Lama had sat and more specifically to a large flat stone on a wooden tray in front of the raised seat.

"It is the stone of Lama Sangwa Dorje. His holy footprint is in the stone ... It is very precious, is a special Buddhist treasure. This stone, the box, the scriptures and yeti scalp, this what monastery is famous for."

Mindhu thanked the monks for letting them stay so long. They giggled and Mindhu pulled gently on Freddie's arm, leading him out into the frozen court-yard.

"I have to be with my brother now, he worries at me. No! *about* me. We stay here tomorrow, to feed the yaks, rest them good so they be strong ... and our Americans, our expedition arrives. Are you be here still – Mr Freddie?"

"Yes … Of course. Yes, I'll see you tomorrow – or will you be busy?"

"Come and see me, after you make your breakfast, with your friends. I will show you something pretty good, Mr Malone."

Her eyes lit up. She inclined her head in a small bow, caught his eye again briefly and then turned on her heels and half-walked, half-ran away through the busy parade ground. Freddie stood by the gates of the monastery staring after her, hating himself because he hadn't been honest. He never could be. How could he, when even *he* didn't know the truth.

"I stopped in the middle of all the tents. I thought I couldn't handle it, you know, if I never saw her again. I knew I had to stay, at least 'til the morning – at least 'til I'd told her the truth about where I was from, and when and everything …"

Just then Freddie found himself outside a large mess tent, used by trekkers to eat and socialise. Now though, there was just the outline of two figures huddled over a table, their silhouettes projected onto the canvas by a storm lantern. He recognised the first voice at once. It was the gruff sound of Mr Cigar Breath. Freddie even thought he could smell cigar smoke. Surely no one could smoke at this altitude, they'd blow their heads off! Actually, he could think of no better outcome for this particular man. He wondered whether the broken 'coconut' inside the temple was a close relative of the bully.

Then the familiar smell of cigar did waft out and was quickly dispersed on the breeze – positive proof it *was* the yeti's relation. Freddie couldn't hear exactly what was being said. He got as close as he dared. Close enough to decide that the exchange was conspiratorial. They were speaking about some valuables they had lost, or mislaid, or couldn't find. Freddie at least found out their names. The yeti's relative was called Callow and his blonde-haired companion was Svensson. Freddie thought it odd that the two men should refer to each other using only their surnames. But then, everything about Callow and Svensson was odd. They stuck out a mile. At any rate, they appeared to have picked the wrong holiday out of the brochure, as neither seemed to be enjoying themselves.

Freddie made a mental note to keep out of their way and not stray into the tented village again. He had a very odd feeling about Callow and Svensson. "I don't like the look of those pirates!" Uncle Patrick would have said. Freddie felt that they were somehow dangerous.

He was greeted like a long lost friend by Lally, who told Ghito to see if they had any food left after realising Freddie was hungry.

"Ah! No one is cook like Ghito," Lally flattered his chef, who beamed a grin and returned with some warmish flatbread and a superb vegetable curry.

His new friends had a big day tomorrow. "No chang tonight!" They would be meeting with the expedition members to make sure everything was in order, or "Shippy shape!" as Lally put it.

Freddie wished them goodnight, and wandered away, unsure of what to do. At least he still had the jacket and sleeping bag, so would be warm and, more importantly, he would see the sun rise once more on Everest, and Mindhu.

No one was out of their canvas confines now as the temperature was plummeting. Freddie found himself back at the monastery gates. An unexpected possibility presented itself almost at once. A scuttling monk emerged from the inner courtyard, head down and shoulders hunched against the night. He was busy closing the wooden shutters of the ground floor windows from the outside by pushing them with a long pole. As he reached the far end, some seventy metres away to Freddie's left, it was easy to slip through the main gates and cross to the inner courtyard. Freddie could see many of the balconies had candles at their windows, but no one would be venturing into the freezing night. Feeling like a commando, Freddie was soon by the temple doors. His mind raced through the options and inching around the left side of the temple wall, guided by shards of moonlight, he made his way to the tiny door he remembered seeing the young tea-pouring monks use during the ceremony.

Freddie leant against the wood and gently turned the heavy metal handle. Bingo! He was in. There was more light inside than he thought there would be. High up in a red holder, a large candle burned. It was reflected in the hundreds of glass mirror pieces that decorated the surrounding statues. Above all of this stood the huge figure of the Buddha with its smiling face. He seemed especially pleased to see Freddie back. The two huge eyes seemed to follow him as he gently pushed the door closed. He moved about cautiously, picking his way through the furniture towards the centre – by the lamas' dais and the cabinet full of treasures.

When his eyes had adjusted to the light, he studied the ancient stone. He could just pick out a tiny footprint much smaller than his own. It was probably all very important, but it didn't really excite him. He was much more impressed by the yeti's scalp, which held his attention for several minutes. He walked around the cabinet to survey it thoroughly from all angles. Then there was the box.

"This is it, Connor. Have you guessed? G.L.M.? This is what it's all about."

Freddie took in Connor's silent shrug. Then he uttered a name: "George Leigh Mallory."

He let it hang in the air.

"Mallory. George Mallory. G.L.M. Come on, Connor! Everest 1922 and '24. You remember? Mallory and Irving might have made the summit in 1924. No one knows. They died, and no one knows. They were last seen well over 28,000 feet up, past the famous gold band on the Tibetan side and heading for glory. In 1924! Dressed in tweeds and long socks."

"His box!" Connor gasped. "His box of ...? Wow!"

"Mindhu said it contained his spirit, because his body had never been found." Freddie was staring at his friend, eyes wide.

"Oh! Wow! Freddie," Connor exclaimed, "you've got Mallory's treasure, and his spirit. Oh, wow!"

Then he stopped dead. "Well, you did have. Now it's in a rubbish bag, in a dump, behind the warden's hut, in the park."

"Yeah – yeah. I know. We'll get it back. I know we will. It's alright. You'll think of something."

Connor had his doubts, but then Freddie said, "Listen. He had a camera. He and Irvine had a camera with them when they attempted the summit of Everest in 1924. It has never been found. If it was, or the film from it was found, it might show whether, you know, whether they got to the top, nearly thirty years before Hillary and Tensing. Can you imagine? Film of Mallory and Irvine on the top of the world in 1924? How important would that be?"

"But what's in the box?" Connor croaked. "Have you looked?"

"No, no, I haven't. At first I was worried about letting his spirit out and it roaming around forever, looking for its owner."

Again, Freddie let the thought float. Then he continued with a knowing smile, "But the thing is, they found Mallory's body. Don't you remember? We did it as part of our project at school. It was frozen solid, high on the mountain. A search party and a film crew found his body in 1999! So that means his spirit can't be in the box anymore, right? Remember, I was in Nepal in 1989, ten years before they discovered Mallory's body in 1999. I couldn't tell Mindhu that Mallory's body would be found ten years later than the date I was there. They'd have locked me up!"

Connor blew out a stream of air.

"This is all getting a bit much for me. How come you've got the box in the first place? I nearly gave it to your mum yesterday. I thought it was her packed lunch."

"You did what?" Freddie spluttered, and at this, both boys dissolved into hysterical laughter.

The sort that hurts. The sort that brings floods of tears to your eyes and cramps your chest. The sort that just when you think you are about to stop and regain control, your friend starts up again and off you both go, harder, louder and more painful than before.

That's how they laughed now, on the warm summer Saturday evening in a wood, high up in an oak tree. A tree that had held many such meetings, though none discussing anything as important as this, and none with such an important outcome hanging in the balance. An outcome which was in the hands of two boys, still aching and shuddering with laughter.

The fate of George Mallory's soul and reputation was currently in the hands of two helpless eejits.

Chapter Thirteen

Freddie made a nest for himself around the back of the Buddha using the rugs and cushions from the lamas' dais and got himself comfortable in the down jacket and sleeping bag. He slept really well until he had a nightmare about Callow and Mindhu getting married. Freddie decided not to doze any longer and risk being found in the temple, so he put everything back in its place.

He stared at the tin box. Supposing there *was* film inside? A pair of smiling faces on top of Everest in 1924. What would it mean to Mallory and Irvine's families? It would turn the history books upside down. Freddie knew the body would be discovered in ten years' time and that it was safe to open the tin to see if it contained film, but he couldn't upset the Nepalese by doing so.

The first horn sounded high up in the monastery and Freddie retreated behind the friendly Buddha. It was easy to slip out once the service was underway, and he was soon sauntering across the parade ground towards the paddock.

He immediately saw the cigar-chewing giant shouting to one of his porters, "Get me some hot water, and be quick about it boy."

Svensson emerged, half dressed and furious.

"Steady, man. Cool it. It's a big day."

Freddie realised Callow was just like a giant, older Jasper, unpredictable and dangerous. But all thoughts of him vanished instantly as there, singing and wiping the faces of her beloved yaks, was Mindhu. Her face lit up as Freddie approached.

"Good morning, Mindhu. I was afraid I was never—"

"We must talk later, Mr Freddie," she cut him off. "We go to our meeting with, how you say, our big man? Bosh. How you say it?"

"Bosh? Oh! *Boss*. Your employers. Em—ploy—ers."

"Em—proy—rers? No! I use *Bosh*. It is easier word. Wait here Mr Freddie."

Ghito and Lally didn't even raise an eyebrow when Freddie arrived and helped himself to a mug of sweet tea and a bowl of porridge. Elvis even gave him seconds and then the entire team went off to their meeting.

Freddie decided he would repay the favour of breakfast by clearing the large mound of washing up. He could see the formal introductions taking place with the American logistics team. They were suntanned and strong. Freddie hoped Mindhu didn't think they looked so impressive.

He finished the last plate as Ghito and Lally returned and thanked him. Freddie bowed and then ran over to Mindhu.

They walked side by side across the meadow in silence. She stopped and looked high up on the mountain in front of them.

"I've got something I need to tell you," Freddie said bravely.

"Yes Mr Malone. Mr brave Freddie. You can talk ... up there."

Freddie followed Mindhu's eye-line. Fifteen hundred or two thousand feet above them was an outcrop of rock, garlanded by fluttering prayer flags.

"Up there? You, err, you want to climb?"

"Yes Mr Malone," she giggled. "Save your breath, you will need it. This is Thyangboche Hill. Is not even proper mountain. We talk there."

Mindhu began skipping up the rocky slope like a mountain goat.

Later, as he sat beside her drinking from a battered water bottle, two hours' climb above Thyangboche, Freddie surveyed the sensational panorama before him. Behind the monastery Mindhu pointed out Khumbila, or the 'Sacred Mountain'. "No one can set foot on. It is sherpa's holy mountain."

She then gestured away to the left. Freddie scanned

the path back down to the shop at Thamserku, then up and along the route back to the hidden Namche Bazaar. To the right, the valley surged all the way to the ring that surrounded Everest. Ama Dhablam, the nearest on the right hand side and in the distance, Pumori, Nuptse, Lhotse, and finally the plumed giant, Sagarmatha.

The water was helping him feel almost human again.

"Thank you." He handed the bottle back. "And thank you," he continued, "for bringing me here ... and thank you for being Mindhu."

She blushed, smiled, and wrinkled her nose in appreciation.

As the prayer flags flapped around them, Mindhu described her ambitions and how impossible they were, whilst she ran the yak trains.

"One day, soon, I will climb mountains, and be 'Mindhu – Sherpana, not Mindhu – yak girl'."

She spoke of her lost brother, Binoi, killed in the Khumbu Icefall – one of the most dangerous parts of Everest.

"Binoi made me laugh, hundred times a day. But when he died, we not laugh in our family for many long time after. My family is given yaks from that expedition, to say sorry for Binoi death. It makes us big rich family, but we rather still have Binoi, and be poor, than have yaks, and be wealthy."

Mindhu's greatest ambition was to climb Everest,

not only for herself, but for her lost brother. They stared at the majestic peak and the huge plume that flew eastwards from its crown. "As a child, I been told it is ... cloud to hide ... Goddess at top of mountain as she washes herself, to hide her nakedness from all the world."

Freddie didn't have the heart to explain to Mindhu that the summit was in the jet stream with 200–300 km per hour winds blowing ice particles from the peak and causing the plume. He knew he possessed the scientific answer, but he much preferred Mindhu's explanation, and he could easily imagine the goddess there now.

Freddie told her only a little of where he lived, slightly more about his family, and a lot about his best mate, Connor. Eventually, he was even brave enough to tell Mindhu that he wished he could stay in Nepal forever.

"One day, I hope you will. Please. You can help me climb the Mother Goddess. We take three prayer scarves. One for Binoi my lost brother, one for the world, and one for ..." She paused and looked at Freddie directly, "for you and me."

Her words took his breath away and he could say nothing for a moment. He stared at the beautiful girl and, without thinking, he replied, "Yes."

They held hands. Simply that. They just held hands and talked and they forgot about the rest of the world.

Freddie knew he could be happy here. Of course he would miss his family and his best friend, but Mindhu was so special, he had to try. Two major problems faced him. Firstly, in Nepal, it was 1989. How would it fit in with time back home? Secondly, he could never be truly honest with Mindhu. He could never tell her everything.

After sharing some bread, Mindhu told Freddie they must make their way down before the temperature dropped. He knew his dream could never be, but a part of him still dared to hope and maybe find a way to make it all work out.

When Freddie and Mindhu arrived back at the camp, preparation was in full swing for the onward journey first thing in the morning. They threw themselves at jobs, trying to make up for their absence during the day.

Freddie said a reluctant goodnight to Mindhu. He had been forced to hand in his kit. One of the bronzed expedition members had raised an eyebrow when he saw Freddie in one of the jackets. To save Lally getting into trouble, Freddie made great show of its safe return, thanking the sirdar loudly, "I really can't thank you enough, Lally. You saved my life after all my equipment was stolen." Lally appreciated the charade and took an equal part in the whole pretence.

Compared to the previous night, Freddie was absolutely freezing. The inside of the temple was the warmest place he was going to find. He had to wait slightly longer for the scuttling monk to close the shutters, but other than this his entry to the temple was remarkably similar to the previous evening.

He took everything from the dais and spent ages trying to build a warm nest, but the chill penetrated no matter how he arranged things. He dozed, he fidgeted, he woke. At one point, he even jogged up and down on the spot to try and warm up.

He dreamt that Uncle Patrick was now the High Lama of Thyangboche and had set up a barbecue, selling yak-dung burgers to trekkers. Elvis was singing *real* Elvis songs, accompanied by the constantly smoking Callow on bongos.

The dream felt so real, Freddie could actually smell cigars. He half woke with the stink still in his nostrils. It was bad enough to dream about them, without smelling them when you woke up. Was that real cigar smoke? No! Don't be stupid. What a ridiculous thought.

He snuggled further into his makeshift cocoon. He even began to feel quite pleasantly cosy, like a wintry night by the radiator. Now Uncle Patrick was rushing round the monastery, shouting and smashing a gong with a burnt sausage on the end of a barbecue fork. Freddie laughed, woke again, coughed and realised that he was now really, quite warm enough.

Actually, he was *too* hot. He pulled aside some of the covers and coughed. This time a tickle stayed at the back of his throat and more coughs followed. Now he felt like he was lying on a beach in Florida. This was much better than earlier on. Who needs fancy sleeping bags and jackets, when you're this wa ... Hold on a minute!

Now Freddie was fully awake. This wasn't right. This wasn't right at all. It should be freezing cold, but he was boiling hot. How?

"Oh! No!" he gasped and coughed violently again. He opened his eyes and saw dancing lights where there should have been darkness.

Then he knew.

The temple was on fire.

He scrambled out of the rugs. There was no need to squint into the gloom to pick out objects now. Everything was very brightly lit by hungry flames. They were fiercest around the dais, but were spreading rapidly and had reached the roof.

Already, a thick layer of black smoke was filling the temple.

Freddie ran to the small side door, before an awful realisation struck him. *The cabinet of treasures!* He fought his way back through the spreading flames. At that moment a beam from the burning roof fell, partially blocking his way. He turned and approached from another angle, coughing and holding his t-shirt over his mouth. He could just make out the cabinet ahead of him. Some of the glass was already smashed.

He dashed forward and tripped up on the wooden tray containing the sacred footprint and fell headlong to the ground amongst the burning embers from the fallen beam. More wood crashed down at his side, showering him with sparks. Freddie knew time was short. He had to grab what he could and head for safety. The noise of the fire was immense and his shouts for help were lost in the ferocious roar of the flames.

He pulled himself to the cabinet and found the parchment already curling with the heat. He grabbed it and laid it down on the stone footprint. Next, he stretched to the top shelf for the yeti's scalp, but it was gone. Then he looked for Mallory's tin. That had vanished too. They must have been knocked out of the cabinet when the first beam fell and the glass had been smashed. He scrabbled around on the floor, but no matter how hard he searched, there was no trace of the precious objects.

Freddie could hardly see now, blinded with tears from the thick smoke. His fingers and palms were getting cut as he scoured the floor. He needed help to find the missing artefacts, but right now, he had to pull the heavy bed of stone and the sacred parchment to safety.

He clawed his way towards the small door, dragging the stone behind him. He was under the thick layer of smoke but in constant danger of being hit by the falling debris that rained down from above. He had about ten metres to go, but it was taking a lifetime because the stone was so incredibly heavy and he had to make several detours around scattered furniture, all of which was now alight. Several times, small explosions blasted burning shrapnel in a thousand trajectories across the huge temple. Twice Freddie had to flick red hot embers off the parchment. If the ancient manuscript survived another five metres it would be a miracle.

He edged closer and closer to the door, still cursing himself for not being able to find the scalp or Mallory's tin box. Splinters tore at his hands. Sparks singed his clothes and his hair. Tears streamed from his eyes. He changed position several times as he dragged the wooden tray and its contents ever closer to safety. Burning debris bounced off him, or stuck to his clothes before being frantically scuffed away. Each time Freddie stopped it was doubly hard to start pulling the massive weight.

He was almost there, but a new panic gripped him. Had he veered off line? He looked around pathetically. He could see nothing. He waved his arm above his head hoping to touch the wall. On he slithered, a few more inches.

There. He'd reached the wall and the wooden door was a step to the left. He made a grab for the handle. The hot metal sizzled against his fingers as he turned it. He pulled with all his remaining strength and as he did so, the rush of fresh air from outside accelerated the flames, but also cleared some of the nearby smoke.

As he turned back to pull the treasures out into the night, he saw the flames roaring around the giant Buddha, lighting his dying face. His eyes were fixed on Freddie, in a final, pitiful look at the world. The paint peeled from his eyeballs, made the once smiling Buddha look like he was crying. Freddie had done his best and he hoped the Buddha would know that.

He collapsed with the scorched tray out into the small courtyard and immediately started shouting, his voice instantly hoarse, due to the amount of smoke he had inhaled.

The fire was spreading rapidly across the whole of the Thyangboche complex. Flames raced through the roof of the temple and to the adjoining courtyards where the monks lived. Burning wooden roof tiles pelted down from the sky, as the mighty ceiling of the temple completely caved in. If it had taken him just ten more seconds to get to the door, he would have been under all that.

The collapse of the roof galvanised Freddie into action once again. He ran around, smashing his bleeding hands on the shutters.

"Fire! There's a fire! Please. Help! Fire! Get out!"

One by one, bleary-eyed monks joined in the battle against the flames, or frantically woke their companions. The huge temple doors had long since been burned from their hinges, but they had fallen outwards, spreading flames to the front of the monastery. Now this area was totally ablaze, preventing any help from entering through the outer gates. People were climbing over the adjoining low wall where the fire hadn't yet reached. But it wouldn't be long before it did.

Trekkers, climbers and porters stood shoulder to shoulder with sherpas, monks and sirdars, fighting the fire, helping the injured and saving what valuables and personal possessions they could. The whole monastery complex was now totally alight. The inferno was almost as bright as day.

Freddie battled back to the tiny inner courtyard which was alight on three sides and found the spot where he had left the treasures. As he bent down to pull the tray, he was hit on the back of the head by a burning roof tile. He was badly dazed, but at least he had stopped it from landing on the parchment.

Freddie was now utterly spent. He sagged down and collapsed over the precious cargo, guarding the relics with his shattered body. If he should die now, at least he would have preserved them for Mindhu and her countrymen. *So that's why I'm really here!* he smiled, realising at last. *Not to save the little girl from the yaks ... but to preserve the teachings ... of Pa ... P* ... The knowledge comforted him as he began slipping peacefully from the world; a world where evil triumphed and the wise and well-meaning were crushed.

In what he calmly assumed to be his final thoughts

before death, Freddie saw the battle between Good and Evil fought out in his mind's eye.

From the depths of his soul, came the surging vision of a beautiful face. Freddie heard her angelic voice singing a sad lament over the body of a boy. A tug of war ensued over his grave, between the melodic angel and a dark, rampaging devil. It was a battle over his fate. Surely this meant Mindhu was nearby somewhere, fighting on his behalf, trying to help him? Maybe she was in danger herself? Did she need him? He had to find out. He felt the will to return flood through his veins.

The radiant vision of Mindhu finally overcame the dark demon. She began hauling Freddie back to safety, giving his exhausted limbs the strength to work again.

He could smell soap and this made him smile.

Freddie woke up with a terrible splutter of sick, missing the priceless sacred parchment by a whisker. He was instantly alert to the desperate situation around him and summoned a surge of effort for one last attempt to survive.

He shouted for help, but all around him was panic and mayhem. Eventually, with the assistance of a reluctant young monk, he hauled the sacred footprint and the historical manuscript through a smouldering corridor and out into the safety of the parade ground.

Freddie handed the brittle parchment to the arm-waving, wizened old monk, who stared open-mouthed, as his earthly and spiritual home blazed out of control, sending flaming splinters of wood hundreds of feet into the night sky.

Freddie was given some water, which revived his strength a little. Having already rescued two of the artefacts, he plunged back into the fire to try and save the rest, but he and several other brave souls were beaten back by the fierce flames.

Defeated, Freddie found himself helping anywhere he could; ferrying water, tending to injuries and burns, moving livestock away from danger and emptying the storerooms before they were consumed by the fire.

The effort was taking its toll on everyone, and the rescue slowed as it became clear that the battle was lost. The mighty building teetered, groaned and sagged to the ground in a hail of sparks.

Most of what could be saved, had been saved.

And all who could be helped, had been helped.

High on a mighty plateau, 12,700 feet above sea level, a fireball warmed the coldest of Himalayan nights. It warmed the faces and bodies of the exhausted rescuers and burned for many hours, until it had nothing left to feed on. "What a terrible price for fuel," a nearby monk whispered to the blood red sky.

It was the nineteenth of January, 1989, and the monastery at Thyangboche was no more.

Chapter Fourteen

As dawn broke, the light from the east gradually became brighter than the flames still dancing amongst the wreckage. Lonely figures picked their way through the remnants of their once magnificent home. Occasionally, someone would stoop and retrieve a pot, or a scorched book. Unbelievably, here and there, some lucky things had survived.

Mindhu tended Freddie. Then, against her advice, he made straight for the area where the temple had once stood, where a hundred shattered timbers still smouldered. All that remained of the mighty Buddha was a badly charred arm, which pointed forlornly at the rapidly thinning ranks of tents on the parade ground.

Freddie found the area where the cabinet of treasures had stood. He could see smashed glass on the floor and moved the layers of crumbling debris aside, searching in vain. The scalp perishing he could understand, even bone would eventually burn – but tin? Surely it would remain as a molten lump somewhere.

Nothing. He stood with his hands on his hips, aching, sore, bleeding, exhausted and sad. He was incredibly sad at the loss of Mallory's treasure – but also because Mindhu's expedition was ready for its onward journey. Freddie knew that this was the worst moment of his life.

Four monks stood on the ridge and sounded their immense horns, summoning people to attend. There, sitting by the sacred stone footprint and Padma's tattered parchments, was the High Lama of Thyangboche. It was the first time Freddie had heard his deep and calming voice. He pointed to the stone, then the parchment, bent and kissed them both, before calling forward the wizened old man, to whom Freddie had entrusted the priceless relics. The old boy spoke to the crowd and threw huge gestures with his arms to the skies and the four points of the compass. He then said something that made them all look at each other and then searchingly around at everyone else.

Then all eyes turned on Freddie. The old man cried out and pointed. Freddie tried to retreat, but was thrust forward towards the High Lama. He stood helplessly in front of the holy man. He had no idea what the old monk was saying. Perhaps he was accusing him of sneaking in and setting light to the temple? He stood, head bowed, expecting arrest, or even worse, at the hands of the angry mob. Still the old man went on. Freddie decided to look up and gauge the mood of the crowd. To his massive relief he saw that the old man was smiling a huge, toothless grin in his direction. Then Mindhu was again by his side translating his words.

"They saying biggest big 'thank you' Mr Freddie, for saving these spe—shul things ... and the lives of all the monks."

She listened to a question from the old man and asked Freddie, "Err! He want to know ... how you help, helped? Who telling you about fire – in temple?"

"Ah! Well, I ... I ... You see I ..." He realised he wasn't giving Mindhu much to translate. He pulled himself together and decided to tell the truth, except for one little white lie.

"I couldn't sleep and I came out of my tent," he gestured vaguely behind him, "and as I was, err, going to y'know," he wafted his other hand at the toilets on the crest of the ridge, "...and I saw smoke from the temple, so I went closer to see what was wrong, but I soon realised it was a big fire. Then I climbed the wall and ... and got into the courtyard. I got into the temple by the small door I had seen the boys use who bring the tea, and I tried to save the treasures. But I couldn't find the yeti scalp, or the tin box, however hard I tried."

Mindhu pointed to his blisters, cuts and burns as proof of the brave act.

"I dragged the stone and the parchments out. Then I carried on shouting and letting people know there was danger. Then I, um, I fainted, I suppose ... and this kind man helped me drag away the sacred footprint and ..." he trailed off.

Mindhu would know what to say. He was totally exhausted. Freddie Malone really didn't feel like being a superhero any more.

Before Mindhu had even finished her version, a massive whooping sound erupted from the large American lady trekker, who beamed and shook Freddie's bleeding hands, causing him to gasp in pain.

"Say boy, you're somethin' else! I betcha one day yoo'll be pres–ee–dent of your li'l ole kern–try."

She hugged him, almost squeezing out what little breath he had left. Mindhu helped prise him free, but only after the khaki giant had insisted on a photo of the two of them together.

"To show all the folks back home. That's li'l ole me, with the future Keeng of En–ger–land." Freddie wanted to correct her and say 'Ireland', but really didn't want to prolong the conversation.

Over a hundred monks were now homeless and several of the small shops that adjoined the monastery were burnt to the ground. One complete line of toilets and wash houses had gone over the cliff and livestock roamed everywhere, their pens destroyed. It would take months and years, maybe even a lifetime to repair the devastation caused by the fire.

An improvised meeting started, so Mindhu was able to smuggle Freddie away. Their camp was now completely stowed on the backs of porters and yaks. Freddie washed his feet in the small stream, then Mindhu bathed his hands and face one last time and explained that she had to leave soon. Freddie nodded gravely, there was nothing he could possibly say. It was, as it was meant to be.

This time he was not ashamed to let Mindhu see he had a tear in his eye.

"I will never forget you. And one day I will come back and see you. I will find you again. One day, Mindhu, I promise."

When Freddie Malone made a promise, it was always kept, but he would definitely have trouble honouring this one.

Mindhu smiled and wiped his next tear away with a gentle finger. She took out a red handkerchief and transferred the drop of liquid to one corner. The handkerchief went dark red where the tear made its mark. She put it to her lips and held it there, as if drinking in his sadness, his love, and his promise.

They sat in silence.

He used Mindhu's soap and comb to smarten himself up, then she brushed her own tangled locks. Freddie solemnly collected the long jet black hairs that stayed in the comb. He carefully coiled the strands and placed them safely in his inside pocket.

Again, they sat in silence. It was comforting, for these last few minutes, just to be together. Neither could really find the right words to express how they felt.

Freddie was about to say thank you to her, but as the words left his mouth, Passang appeared and coughed politely, as if knocking on some imaginary door. Mindhu stood and gathered her pack. Passang then joined the front of the yak train heading the expedition. He called in a firm voice and pulled at the leading yak, who grudgingly gave way. Beast after beast trundled past them, some saluting the heroic deeds of Freddie Malone with stringy wet snorts, others simply looking at the barefoot boy with mild curiosity. Freddie never wanted the procession to end.

They stood side by side, unable now to look at each other.

Then as a final brown yak heralded the last of the line, Mindhu stepped silently towards him, half stretched on tiptoe and kissed Freddie Malone on the cheek. She joined the back of the shaggy train and began the long walk out of his life.

"Namaste," he managed, with a quivering voice.

Then the porters passed him, all wanting to shake his hand and bid him farewell. This included the cheeky one, who pretended to cry, then said, "Cheers." Then came a subdued Elvis, who seemed very badly shaken by the fire; Mingma nodded politely, already half looking ahead at Sagarmatha. Then Saylor, wearing every single layer of clothing and with the toilet seat in pride of place on top of his load once more; Ghito, polite and half bowed; and finally Lally, who hugged Freddie fiercely and moved swiftly on, upright and firm, in charge once more.

All made their 'namastes' and all inflected them differently. But for every 'Namaste' that Freddie returned, it was as if another nail was hammered into the wall being built between him and Mindhu.

He watched her slowly getting smaller and smaller as the smart, brave climbers of the expedition were passing with their sherpa guides. A few said, "Hi, kid," but Freddie only replied with, "Namaste." It was the only word to sum up his feelings. It was the best word. It always would be.

Freddie saw the last yak disappear up and over a ridge in the distance. As it did so, a small figure turned and waved a tiny red dot of a handkerchief in his direction. He waved his arms in return and realised that, not for the first time in his short life, he had his socks in his hands. This time though there was no embarrassment and a smile danced briefly on his lips. The tiny figure finally disappeared and Freddie sagged to the ground.

Freddie decided to climb Thyangboche Hill to clear his head and work out what he must do to get home again. The hill seemed the best place, as the day before he had spent his happiest ever moments there. Every minute or so, he nervously checked to make sure Mindhu's raven locks were safely stored in his pocket.

After an hour of half-hearted climbing, he gave up. He had wanted to reach the point he and Mindhu got to yesterday, but his heart just wasn't in it, and anyway, "That sort of thing only happens in films," he said to himself.

He had still managed to climb quite high and had a perfect view of the wreckage of Thyangboche. The burnt beams sticking up from the ground looked like the ribs of a long-dead dinosaur.

Freddie's gaze stretched to the ruins where the tin box should have been. The remains of the giant Buddha lay scattered and steaming, with only the huge arm surviving. In a curious way, because only one finger remained intact, it seemed that the Buddha was pointing at something.

Freddie followed the line of the outstretched finger and as quickly and painfully as a jab from Jasper, a lightning bolt seared through his brain.

"That's it!" Freddie gasped aloud. Everything suddenly made sense. It was like a million locks turning at once, a million doors opening and a million lights switching on, revealing the final answer.

"How stupid have I been?" Freddie shook his head in disbelief.

"What? ... What? Tell me, Freddie!" Connor pleaded. "What lights? What doors? You must have left something out. What locks? Aarrgghh. Tell me!" Connor shifted towards his best friend and nearly lost his balance on the branch.

"Come on, Connor. We've got to get back to the park," Freddie said.

The sky had lost its brightness as the evening settled in. They clambered down from the oak and left the darkness of the wood. It was time to retrieve Mallory's box.

"Talking of mountains," a desperate Connor prompted the storyteller.

Freddie smiled.

"I bet if I gave you five more minutes, you'd guess."

Connor frowned and then shook his head. "Just tell me. Please."

"Alright, alright!" Freddie cleared his throat dramatically. "The Buddha's arm, remember? Well, it looked like the finger was pointing through the ruins towards ... Callow and Svensson. They were about to leave. It was like the Buddha was trying to tell me it was them. Remember the cigar smoke in the temple?"

"What? You mean they broke into the temple

and stole the thingies?"

"You got it."

"And started the fire, to cover that the treasures were stolen."

"That's it."

"They'd have to make it look like they were destroyed, not taken."

"Bingo. But I couldn't just walk up and accuse them. What if I was wrong? I had no proof. Then I noticed they both wore these bags around their waists – easily big enough to fit the stolen things in. Whenever I caught up with them, I'd start my search with them. But, Connor, which direction would they go? Towards Everest, or Namche Bazaar? Would they stay with their group on their trek, or splinter off and make their escape?"

Freddie found himself overlooking the devastation and suddenly smiling. Once again he was a boy with a mission. Luckily that mission meant staying in this wonderful place a while longer.

Something strange was happening in front of the ruins. There was an argument going on between a local sirdar and Callow. It seemed a parting of the ways was occurring. Angry shouts wafted up to Freddie from a few hundred feet below.

"... *when* I want!" Callow barked.

The sirdar was pointing towards Everest. Callow

was pointing down to Namche. Was this because they had got what they came for?

"I don't care if it does leave you short of porters. They're coming with us."

Then the two villains threw their daypacks onto their shoulders and ushered the confused porters ahead of them, laden with tent and kit bags belonging to the pair.

Freddie watched like a hawk. The party of four made their way past what was left of the monastery. As they did so, Callow lit a cigar and turned to Svensson. They exchanged slaps on the back and high fived each other. Not the sort of behaviour you would expect from people who had just witnessed such devastation.

Freddie needed a plan. He had to catch up with them, steal the artefacts back, and return them to Thyangboche. He had to remain invisible, but keep right on their heels. Most importantly, he had to succeed.

Callow turned to Svensson and smugly patted the bag fastened around his waist in an arrogant parting gesture. No one saw him, except Freddie Malone. No one else would have understood, even if they had seen. Then the destroyers of Thyangboche Monastery disappeared over the ridge and out of sight.

"I've figured it out!" Freddie gasped.

Freddie Malone stood on the high mountain flank with his eyes tightly shut and vowed that he would do his best to complete his mission. A vision of Uncle

Patrick flashed through his mind, spurring him on. He felt encouraged and comforted by what seemed like his uncle's support and allowed his eyes to stray one last time to the path which led to Everest.

Then he uttered a passionate vow: He would succeed in his quest and return the stolen relics for the sake of a beautiful girl. A beautiful girl who, surprisingly, was herself no stranger to stealing – for recently she had stolen something precious. His heart.

Chapter Fifteen

Freddie passed groups of troubled monks trying to work out what to do for shelter. Now, nearly two hundred people in Thyangboche had nowhere to live. Officials drew up lists, as everyone had to be accounted for. Freddie saw the footballing monks despatched in the direction Mindhu had taken, the ever present giggles now long gone.

As people began their journeys away from the smouldering plateau, they filed past the High Lama and either shook his hand or kissed his long robes as near to the ground as they could.

Callow and Svensson had not just stolen two valuable relics, they had forced a whole community to its knees. It would take years to rebuild their lives. Even then, things would never really be the same.

Freddie couldn't help scouring the ruins one last time, but a hand touched him lightly on the shoulder, and as he turned, he came face to face with the gentle smile of the High Lama of Thyangboche.

"They are gone, my good friend. Our treasures are gone. We will find more treasures one day to replace them. After all, they are only things. Important things, I know – but just things. We still have our greatest gifts – the holy stone and the teachings of Padma. However, my young friend, people matter too and I am worried about you. When are you leaving with your friends for safety?"

"I'm going now, sir. I just thought, y'know, I'd have one more look."

"Thank you, my friend. But now you must think of yourself and your companions, and not us, or our problems. They are a test for us and not you. You will have your own tests in life and sadly we will not be there to help you."

The High Lama of Thyangboche placed a thin white silk prayer scarf around Freddie's neck, and in that moment Freddie knew he would do anything to return the relics to their rightful place. However frightened he was of Callow and Svensson, he vowed that he would succeed, not only for Mindhu, but for all these wonderful people.

"Thank you, sir. I'll tell everyone about the fire when I get home, and I promise I'll send some … some *thing*, to help restore your beautiful monastery."

"Namaste." The holy man spoke the word slowly

and finally.

Freddie walked away. He could not bear to look back as he stood on the ridge. He wanted to remember Thyangboche as he had first seen it.

Eight long, hard hours later he rested his aching limbs on the sparse hillock where he had first encountered this magical kingdom. He had not overtaken Callow and Svensson yet and doubts again crowded his weary mind as to whether he was doing the right thing. He forced himself to remain positive.

As he stood to continue on to Lally's hut for some much needed rest and sleep, a sudden breeze picked up and Freddie's gaze was drawn to a particular spot just to the side of the path. Before his eyes, a shimmering watery outline began to appear. No. It couldn't be. Freddie blinked and looked again. It was the homeward portal reforming. Freddie took a few steps towards it. The outline became clearer and appeared more permanent, as the numbers began to dance and revolve, as if making their mind up at which date they wanted to settle. Freddie was mesmerised. It was so enticing. Instead of the frightening cacophony of noise he remembered from his arrival, soothing voices beckoned him to enter the fluid portal and return home. It was incredibly tempting, almost like the ancient sirens luring sailors onto the rocks.

Freddie hesitated. He had not completed his

mission. He could not leave the mystery unsolved. He must carry on and do battle with Callow and Svensson. He could never live with himself if he returned home now to his comfortable and easy life. How could he ever enjoy his sausage, mash and peas knowing a nation mourned for their lost treasures? He wanted justice. He wanted to avenge the displaced inhabitants of the once beautiful monastery.

He was struck by panic at the thought that this might be his only chance of returning home, but felt calmer when he reasoned that if it had appeared once to him, it would do so again. Surely he would just have to return here after solving the mystery, and step through the welcoming frame?

The portal tried to draw him in, but Freddie dug his huge boots into the turf and leaned his weight backwards like the captain of a tug-o-war team. He could see through the shimmering open portal now into the vortex beyond. Ghost-like friendly figures crowded the entrance, beckoning him back. Freddie's mind began changing again as he thought of his mum and dad and the worry they must be going through over his disappearance. What must they be thinking? It would take a lifetime of pocket money to repair the damage to his bedroom wall. How would he explain everything?

Just then, a figure with his back to Freddie shepherded the pleading figures away from the opening.

Freddie couldn't see his face, but even dressed as he was, in a cloak, he bore an amazing resemblance to his favourite uncle. Then the portal started to fade and Freddie watched the clear outline recede. The moment to leave had well and truly passed.

Exhausted, Freddie fell heavily to the ground as the gravitational pull of Nepal overtook the magnetism of the vortex. It was all too much for a thirteen-year-old to cope with and Freddie gave way to great shoulder-shaking sobs of wretchedness. It only lasted two minutes. His misery was overtaken by severe cold and he pulled himself together. *Get warm, get fed, get watered.*

Inside Lally's hut again, covered in every article he could lay his freezing hands on, Freddie finally lay down and slept. He had to be ready for whatever might surprise him in his quest. The High Lama's prayer scarf, worn proudly round Freddie's neck, would surely protect him against any evil. It was a comforting thought.

Freddie did rest and sleep, but he dreamt of fire, destruction and smoke. Cigar smoke! He awoke in a panic, expecting to see Callow standing over him and was relieved to find the only other occupant was the small smiling Budha.

Emerging into the cold dawn, he was determined to see the first movements of human traffic towards the airstrip at Luckla, the vital link to the outside world. If he didn't see the arsonists in Namche, he would race on to Luckla and wait for them there. He knew they would choose to fly out, rather than opt for a further six-day trek to the nearest road. Callow and Svensson didn't strike him as people who'd want to walk much further than they had to.

Freddie was among the first refugees to reach Namche from Thyangboche. He passed the stupa and stood at the edge of the precipice. The only path away from Namche was immediately to his left. A sheer drop into oblivion lay in front, beyond a line of metal posts acting as a poor deterrent to anyone falling after too much chang. He strained his eyes for movement on the path. A few porters were making their way up, but he could see no groups of four walking down.

What were his options? He could sit tight here, where he wouldn't miss anyone, or he could gamble and go to Tara's café. He would still be able to see everyone that passed through the town if he sat outside.

As he got to his feet, the long-forgotten coins from the Indian takeaway jangled in his pocket. He remembered the bank offering to change foreign currency. It was worth a try.

Freddie claimed a place third in line outside the brightly painted green and pink bank. He scoured the faces of all who passed, pretending to be an interested observer. The queue was alive with talk about the fire

163

in Thyangboche, as the elderly couple in front and the growing number behind Freddie told of what they had seen from the crest of the cliff above the town.

From the number of people working in the square, it was obvious some sort of reception centre was being set up. A large marquee was near completion. The roof was already in place and two men were unrolling and hanging the side panels.

The wooden door of the bank creaked open and a small, friendly-looking man in a shirt and tie welcomed his customers.

The elderly couple ahead obviously liked to use their bank visits to catch up on local gossip, so it was ten minutes before Freddie was served. He spoke slowly and clearly and was surprised to be replied to in perfect English.

"I understand you perfectly, sir. I have in fact been to England. I was a Gurkha soldier, sir. I lived in your wonderful country for many happy years."

"Oh right. I ... I see," stuttered Freddie.

"Do you know Folkestone, in Kent? It's where I was based with the Gurkha regiment. There's a lovely pub in Sandgates, The Ship. Is it still there? Does it still serve warm beer?"

"Ah! Yes, probably, but I'm too young to go into pubs, so I don't know."

"Of course, of course, how silly of me. How is London, then? Does Big Ben still chime? Is the Lord

Nelson still standing proud on his column? Does the great Mother Thames still wind like a friendly snake?"

"Yes, yes and yes," replied Freddie with a smile.

"All a very long way from Namche Bazaar, my young friend. A very long way indeed." His eyes drifted to the window through which the peak of Thamserku was perfectly framed. "But Namche has its compensations. It is not such a bad place to end one's days."

"I can't think of anywhere better," Freddie agreed. "I have just come from Thyangboche. Things are very bad up there. Will everyone be all right?"

"Aah! Now, sir, I don't know. We will do all we can. We are collecting money and goods to help with their welfare. But please, tell me, were the sacred scripts of Padma saved from the flames?"

"Yes. Err, yes! I think they survived the fire. Yes, I'm sure they did actually. I remember seeing them," Freddie stammered.

"Oh! I am mightily relieved, I really am. They are so important."

"Good," muttered Freddie. The queue shuffled behind him.

"I'm sorry. I'm holding things up. May I exchange some money? English sterling into – Nepalese err …"

"Rupees, sir, rupees."

"Yes, of course. Nepalese rupees."

"How much would you like to change? And can I see your passport please?"

"Ah, I, err, I haven't got my passport. It's still on its way with my parents, from Thyangboche. I've come on ahead to try and get somewhere to stay."

"I see, I see, sir." Freddie waited while the cashier pondered the situation. "How much did you say you wanted to change?"

"Six pounds … in coins, new coins, six pounds exactly, if that's not too much? And I would like to give half of it to the fund, to help the refugees from the monastery."

"Six new pounds you say, sir. Oh my goodness, things change so fast."

The man consulted a table of figures and looked back at Freddie.

"I'm sure I can help you to that amount. You're not exactly going to break the bank."

As the friendly cashier counted out two piles of notes, one for Freddie and one for the relief effort, he spoke in a loud voice to the rest of the queue, indicating the second pile of notes and Freddie's generosity. Freddie received a round of applause. He blushed, bowed his head, and thanking the kind ex-Gurkha, collected his money and repeated, "Namaste," all along the queue.

He was almost at the door, when the man called after him, "Give my love to the Queen when you see her."

Freddie turned and said, "I certainly will. Thank

you. Namaste."

No sooner had he stepped from the shade of the bank into the glare of the street, than his senses screamed **RED ALERT**.

Chapter Sixteen

A thin layer of grey cigar smoke hung above the heads of the busy shoppers. Freddie looked downhill to the square, waiting for the telltale puff to rise. He didn't have to wait long. A freshly exhaled plume pinpointed Callow's position a hundred metres ahead. Freddie only moved to follow once he could also see Svensson.

Just play it cool. Follow from a distance. Wait for the right moment. Retrieve the lost treasures. Take them back to where they belong, and go home. Bingo.

Simple, when you say it like that.

He shadowed them down the street until they emerged into the square and made straight for the huge marquee. An elderly Nepalese man was standing at the entrance, taking people's details. He nodded gravely as Callow and Svensson reached the front of the queue. Freddie, who was four behind, listened to the familiar gruff tones.

"We need some hot food, then we'll get the hell out of here."

"May I offer my sincere condolences that your trek has been so disrupted. I can assure you that the people of Namche will do all we can to hel—"

"Yeah! Whatever! Where's the food?" Callow barked.

The man recoiled, but regained his composure and pointed into the marquee. He was still a little shaken by the time Freddie found himself at the front of his second queue of the morning.

"Good morning, sir," Freddie started. "I only need to wash and a cup of tea, and maybe a small bowl of rice to see me through, if that's not too much trouble." He found himself being twice as polite as usual to make up for Callow's rudeness. Once inside, Freddie made himself as invisible as possible. He washed, drank, ate, and observed his quarry, who were sitting by themselves, having abandoned their porters outside.

Callow and Svensson appeared largely oblivious to everything around them. They were washing their feet, changing socks and only occasionally glancing around. They had a confident air about them, as if they had achieved what they had set out to do. Job done, and in the bag – literally.

"Get me another shirt will you. Huh? You speak English? Shirt? I – Need – Shirt. You understand?" Callow turned back to Svensson, who was now busy unbuckling his bumbag. "These people, jeez!"

Freddie felt every fibre of his body tingle. He took deep breaths to calm himself. Then a bustling old lady put some rank-smelling gel on Freddie's face to help with his blisters and burns. This was perfect cover, as he could observe through the gap under her nursing arms.

Freddie watched the shadows of the two tent men passing slowly along the outside of the gently billowing canvas. They had hung the side walls of the marquee and were now methodically joining them and tying them down, one on each side, making their way round to behind where Callow and Svensson were sitting. Freddie calculated that if they continued at this rate, they would meet at the far end of the marquee, right behind the villains, where there was also the final gaping side flap to secure.

Freddie had a plan.

Svensson had already removed his bumbag. It was on the table. Callow would have to remove his to change his shirt. Next to where the pair were sitting, the tent panel still had to be laced up, but this would happen very soon now. Freddie felt the critical moment arriving. His mouth went dry.

He wouldn't do anything unless he was absolutely certain of success. It was too risky. He knew there would be other opportunities, maybe at night-time. Perhaps he'd steal the bags while the temple robbers slept? His only plan, if caught, was to open the bumbags, reveal the stolen relics and have Callow and Svensson arrested. But what if the bumbags just held personal items? What if the yeti's scalp and Mallory's tin were not there? What if they were in the kit bags that their porters guarded outside? What then?

The plan desperately needed more work. He might only get one chance, so had to make it count. He had one huge advantage though – surprise. But the longer this all went on, the more likely they were to spot him. He must strike sooner rather than later.

A young man approached Callow with a large blue checked shirt. Callow tutted loudly, addressing the volunteer as if he was a four year old. "This all you got, pal? Oi! I'm talking to you. This – The – Only – Colour?"

The young man shrugged apologetically and retreated.

The old lady finished with Freddie and, after thanking her, he got up and ventured nearer to the middle of the marquee. He now had a clear line of approach.

Callow scanned the tent and Freddie dropped down to tie his bootlaces. He slowly raised his eyes again and saw Callow unbuckling his bumbag, placing it delicately on the table next to Svensson's.

Surely Freddie's moment had arrived. The tent peggers were closing in on the gap that was his only escape route. Once the panel was laced up, this plan was history. He crouched down like an athlete in the starting blocks, checking his laces. It would all depend on whether Callow changed his shirt now, or waited. If he waited, the opportunity would be gone.

Callow unbuttoned his old maroon top. Too slowly, surely. The tent peggers were only two panels away either side of the gap. Svensson was nearly ready to put his bag back on. The critical moment was approaching. Then …

Callow's shirt went up over his head. Svensson was buttoning his last cuff, the tent peggers moved to the last tie before the gap – and Freddie bolted like an Olympic sprinter.

He was at the table before anyone realised. He grabbed both bags just as Svensson made a move for his. Freddie darted around the back of Callow, who still had his top stuck over his head and made for the gap in the side of the tent. With his spare hand, Freddie spun the off-balance Callow into the path of the advancing Svensson, who was cursing Freddie and shouting, "Oi! You little …"

An almighty confusion followed as Freddie leapt through the unlaced side of the tent. Callow, still with his shirt wedged over his head, prevented Svensson from getting out. Not only that, but the tent peggers, stunned by Freddie's sudden eruption, stood baffled, blocking the gap. They were roughly thrown aside as the robbed robbers burst through and out of the marquee.

Freddie ran like the wind across the square with shouts flying behind him. He felt exhilarated. He'd done it. He ran and ran, with the two bumbags safely clutched in one hand as he made for ... Ah! As he made for the ... That was the problem. He hadn't thought of where to go.

Everything else had been planned and calculated, except how to escape. Svensson and the bare-chested Callow were lumbering after him across the square, closing rapidly now that Freddie had stopped. He was like a rabbit caught in headlights, searching left and right for an exit. He backed away from his assailants towards the stupa, as the whole population of Namche descended on him, led by two very angry, wild-eyed men. He had to think of something, fast.

His original plan had been to casually return the relics to the High Lama, marry Mindhu, start a yak dung business and live happily ever after. Now he had less than five seconds to expose the villains and save his life.

Freddie couldn't run down the path out of Namche; he would be caught in a flash, and, anyway, it was blocked by advancing villagers. He couldn't run up through the town either – the main street was packed. It would be like trying to swim through mud.

All the time Callow and Svensson closed in on

Freddie. They were now just twenty paces away. Freddie shouted and began to undo one of the bumbags to reveal the relics. "Listen! Please! Listen to me! These two men stole the ..."

His words were drowned out by the furore around him, not least from the approaching villains. Freddie's small voice was lost in the clamour. It was useless. No one could hear him. However loud he screamed, their raging shouts drowned his desperate pleas. They would grab back their bounty and he would be hauled away to face the law, unable to prove he was telling the truth.

Now they were almost upon him. Freddie could feel the shock waves of Callow's furious tirade. Freddie had backed up right to the edge of the chasm. His boots were literally on the crumbling edge of the cliff. Callow made a desperate lunge for the bags. As Freddie swung them out of reach, he lost his balance and slipped. One boot slithered on the coarse gravel and plunged over the drop. Both men made a grab for Freddie and the bags, but all of Freddie's weight and momentum took him away from their clutches. This arc not only took him away from his attackers, but also away from the crumbling lip and he began to fall. He did all he could to scrabble a handhold on the passing cliff edge, but it was useless.

Callow and Svensson's outstretched arms flailed at him as he dropped away from them. Freddie heard their desperate shouts and saw their anger change to disbelief and bewilderment. He saw the ring of villagers arrive at the edge and stretch out their arms in desperate attempts to help. He registered the distress on their faces, some turning away, unable to watch, covering their heads with their hands. Their screams of anguish mixed with the final raging agony of Callow, as his treasure was lost. All the while, Freddie fell away from the cliff edge in a perfect arc. These then, were the last few moments of his short courageous life.

Suddenly, everything went absolutely quiet. No pounding of feet across the dusty market square. No spit and thunder from his angry pursuers. There was a simple and total serenity, as Freddie lay flat in the air and dropped.

And dropped.

And dropped.

For a second or two he was transfixed by the sheer beauty of the valley beneath him and the exhilaration of feeling like he was flying. This was replaced by thoughts of home and a vision of his grieving parents, not ever knowing the fate of their son. He thought of Connor, struggling on alone against Jasper. He thought of Mindhu, finding out about his death but knowing that he had retrieved the relics. He thought of Uncle Patrick, cheering as he recited his birthday challenge.

Of course. That's how I'll die, Freddie reasoned.

Before Freddie even realised what he was doing,

he began to try and recite 'If—'. But he was facing downwards and the air was rushing into his mouth. He just could not force the words out. As he opened his lips, the wind forced his cheeks into crazy rippling movements, impossible to control.

Still he fell.

"If you" sounded like "Iwww ywww." That was no good. Freddie attempted to turn upwards, but ended up spinning end over end, in a crazy and haphazard tumble. He spread his arms to try to regain control. The head over heels motion instantly stopped. Good. Try again.

"Iwfw Ywowuw …"

Useless! He had to spin sideways. What if he tucked one arm in? Anything was worth a try.

The bumbags ripped away, remaining with him only because they had looped themselves around his neck. Freddie trapped them against his chest with his chin.

'Think, Freddie. Think. It can't end like this!'

He tried to grab the vital cargo, but the rushing stream of air made it impossible to do *what* he wanted, *when* he wanted.

Flashing images of the bank cashier waving at the queen, Saylor's toilet seat and Mindhu's hair zapped around his mind. People say when you die your life passes before you. Was this *it*? Was this his life? The last of the fleeting figures to pop up was Uncle Patrick. "Pull yourself together, boy," his Uncle shouted. "Don't give in! You've got *ME* on your side."

Freddie shot out his arm. The wind buffeted his fist against his jaw, but he managed to grab onto the straps of both bags. *So. Now. Recite the poem. That is all.*

"If … you …"

How long had he been falling?

"Concentrate!" he screamed at himself. *Think only of the poem.* "If … you … can …"

He had to get through it. On he went. On and on as he hurtled downwards. On and on. *Keep going. Only a few words to go.*

"Six–ty se–conds worth – of dis–tance run …"

The ground was rising up to meet him now as he plunged downwards. With every revolution he uttered a word and was fifty feet closer to the raging torrent of the river below and to his certain death.

"THEN … YOU'LL … BE … A … MAN … MY … SON!"

There. He had finished. And still he fell. Why did dying take so long? He rushed headlong towards a whirlpool in the bubbling meltwater.

Freddie turned one last time, stuck out his arms, with the bumbags safely hooked round his neck, and decided he would dive into the water head first, to end it all quickly. It would all be over in a few seconds. They would find his body and the relics, and realise that he had done a good thing. Mindhu would be proud of him. That was what he cared about more than anything.

He focussed on her face, with the red handkerchief held against her cheek and uttered the only word that seemed appropriate in the circumstances

"NA ... MAS ... TE ..."

As the ground rose up to meet him, the rushing wind of his descent suddenly ceased. Freddie's fingertips pierced the surface of the icy water as everything suddenly turned into slow motion. Instead of meeting his end, which he had been totally prepared for, Freddie entered the tunnel and found himself screaming full pelt, back along the vortex.

By a twist of fate he was not prepared to examine at any great length, in case it decided to reverse its decision, he was still alive.

Freddie was buffeted by the walls and curled himself up into a ball to protect the bumbags. Was it the poem that had saved him? Uncle Patrick had said it would help him throughout his life. He hurtled and bounced past the other portals along the tunnel, like giant adverts displayed opposite London underground platforms. A huge collage of everyone he'd ever met flashed across his mind's eye, smiling and hugging, shouting and dancing.

Eventually Freddie felt himself slowing down, little by little. By the time his nose was pressed against the wall at the end of the tunnel, he had only just ground to a shuddering halt.

His whole body screamed with pain. In fact, it ached

all over so badly that he could identify no part that felt normal. Freddie laughed like a madman, unable just at that moment to come to terms not only with the last few minutes, but his entire experience. The relief was indescribable.

Freddie clung to the wall. Was his bedroom on the other side? He made a tiny slash in the gel-like material with his belt buckle, wincing as he fumbled with his injured hands. Freddie peered through the tear, saw his bedroom and with another flood of relief, half fell and half dropped through the wall. He entered via the poster of the planets, not a million miles away from Neptune, which was exactly where he felt he had returned from.

There was a loud, almost soggy plop as the poster closed behind him. It rippled and then solidified, leaving the wall completely unblemished, as if nothing at all had happened.

Freddie lay on his bedroom floor, dazed and bewildered. The first thing he did was check his inside pocket, feeling frantically for the knot of raven black hair. "Yes!" He held the coiled strands in front of his watering eyes and kissed them gently.

It was over. He was safe, and he was home.

In the gathering gloom of a balmy English summer night, the boys turned the corner by the park, as Freddie finally fell silent. His story told.

Connor shook his head in bewilderment, trying to form a sentence that could in any way follow what he had just heard. Eventually he uttered the simplest of observations:

"Well, that would explain why your eyes were bloodshot!"

Chapter Seventeen

Freddie and Connor turned their attention to retrieving the relics. That they should have survived so much to end up lost in a pile of public refuse was unbelievable.

Freddie borrowed Connor's phone to ring his parents. Connor had ten missed calls, which meant one of them was in trouble. It was Freddie. He should have been home hours ago, his mum told him. Freddie hung up, looking stunned.

"Mollie's having her baby, in Cornwall. I've got to go. My parents want to drive down tonight, y'know, to be with her."

Connor nodded slowly, shifting uneasily from foot to foot.

"What shall we do about the tin and the yeti's head?"

"Scalp," said Freddie absent-mindedly. "Yeti's

scalp."

"Yeah! Sorry, scalp! But what shall we do?"

Freddie thought for a second.

"You've got to get the treasures, Connor. You've got to rescue them and keep them safe until I get back. It's up to you! And when I get back from Cornwall we'll both try and go back through the vortex, back to Nepal. Let's go together, so you can meet Mindhu, and Elvis and … How long does it take to have a baby?"

Connor and Freddie looked at each other blankly.

"My dad has to come back for work anyway. Mum's going to stay with Mollie for a bit. I'll come back with my dad. Listen, Connor, find the treasures and keep them safe – and don't open the tin, whatever you do. Please! Don't. Open. The. Tin. There may be film in there, and if it's exposed to the light, it'll be ruined."

"Yes, of course." Connor tried to sound confident. "I'll try, Freddie."

They walked on swiftly in silence.

"Can't you just help me find the bag and then go?" Connor pleaded.

Freddie shook his head. "My parents are on their way to pick me up now. We're driving straight to Port Isaac." As he spoke, headlights picked them out through the gathering dusk.

"Remember, Connor," Freddie said. "It's up to you. You have to succeed. You're the only hope. I'll ring every day. What time?"

"Err, whenever. I'm not sure. Aghh! Freddie – what if …?"

"Good evening, Connor," said Mr and Mrs M, through the opening car window.

"Hello … err, Hi! Sorry. It's all my fault. I didn't have my phone on."

It was their joint policy to take the blame in front of the other one's parents. If truth be told it was a slightly one-sided arrangement, as Freddie never had to take *any* blame.

Freddie slotted into the back seat, in a sort of nest among the cases, toys and food and … whatever else you take to someone who's just about to have a baby.

Whilst Mrs M made Connor show her his bruises, Freddie strapped himself in and was handed sandwiches and a drink from a coolbag by his dad. He gave Connor a thumbs up, and then put his hand to his ear, mouthing, "I'll ring you."

"Please say hello to Mollie for me, and good luck and stuff."

"I will, Connor, thank you, how thoughtful of you. Thanks indeed. You're a brave an' darlin' boy," said Mrs M. "Get home safely, now." And with that they sped away.

Connor couldn't believe it. One moment he was flying headlong off a cliff with Freddie, and the next he was left to save the most sacred and valuable treasures in the world – by himself. At least, that was how it felt. A sudden feeling of loneliness hit him. He wasn't used to being in charge. He stared at the sign by the park entrance. It said: 'Summer Opening Times – Dawn to Dusk.'

Connor could see the large park keeper touring around on his bike, padlocking gates, but the main entrance was still open. He headed cautiously for the hut and the mesh-fenced waste dump behind it. In the fading light, the bright interior of the hut shone out, illuminating the side and the back.

Connor was not really prepared for the sight that confronted him. Throughout the long hot day a mountain of black bin bags had been amassed. The smell was unbelievable. He slipped into the compound easily but could only just make out the back wall. He could see a television flickering, so the park guys weren't going home just yet. That meant the light would be on for a few more minutes.

Connor knew roughly where he was heading and tried to be as quiet as possible, timing his noisier movements with bursts of nearby traffic.

"Ah! Brilliant."

There was the metal fence bracket sticking up. He worked his way towards it. The smell all around was utterly rank. His foot had gone through a bag and he'd now got a wodge of squidgy, rotting banana on his shoe, which stank. Then a fatty, barbecue type of smell quickly followed. Then nappies. Nappies everywhere. Connor was starting to feel really sick. Lots of nappies, really, lots and lots of them.

He couldn't help but make *some* noise, because the bags had so many empty cans in them. He froze as the silhouette of the larger park keeper entered the hut and closed the door. Connor could see the two of them watching television as he peered over the high barricade of bags he'd made to hide what he was up to.

He was getting filthier by the second. He moved the newest bags away from the back wall and added them to the barricade. Now he could begin his search.

There were about ten or fifteen bags he had to go through. If the treasures weren't in those, he was really lost.

The first bag he opened had an old tea towel in it. He tied it round his nose and mouth to form a barrier against the smell. No relics though. He was never going to be that lucky. Connor reckoned they would be in the ninth or tenth bag. So when he drew a blank with the second, third and fourth sacks, all of which contained items festering since the morning, he wasn't too downhearted. The rubbish was still warm from the sun and he was soon covered with melted ice cream, cheese, chewing gum and the last dregs of drink from cans. It really was horrible. He stupidly ran his fingers through his sweaty hair to push it out of his eyes and felt something sticky lodge there.

Connor had to stop dead still before opening the sixth bag, as the younger park keeper headed off, laughing over his shoulder, "G'night, Trev. Enjoy the show."

Connor was now covered from head to toe in sticky, hot, smelly gunge and he cursed Freddie. "It's alright for him," he mumbled, "a cosy car with sandwiches and ..."

"This what you're lookin' for?"

Connor's heart leapt into his mouth. He spun around as a torch beam speared into his eyes. The large park keeper stood blocking the way to freedom. He was trapped.

Connor's whole world crashed. Not only had he let Freddie down, he had let down Mindhu, the monks at the monastery and everyone in Nepal. All he had to do was find two things in a bin bag, and he couldn't even do that properly. Why hadn't he waited until midnight, or three o'clock in the morning? He felt *so* stupid and angry with himself. He shielded his watering, frightened eyes.

"Well?" said the keeper. "Is this what you're looking for?" He held up a plastic bag. A blue and white striped carrier bag, just like the one Freddie had dumped in the bin that morning.

"Come out of there, slowly. I don't want any trouble from you. Don't worry, I'm not going to hurt you, boy."

Connor couldn't really believe his ears. What was he saying? Why was he holding Freddie's carrier bag?

"We've been watching you, me and Jezzer." He smiled and raised the torch beam high up over the compound to a security camera which was pointing straight at Connor.

"Infrared. It's a wonderful thing. I must say, you've been very tidy. You've moved the bags nearer for the truck in the morning. Very considerate of you."

He spoke in a deep, lumbering voice, which went exactly with his large belly and bushy moustache. His eyes were kind though, and he seemed to be enjoying himself.

"Don't worry, boy. You're like me. I saw what went on this morning. I'm not stupid. I used to have a lot of trouble from gangs when I was a lad. What's yer name?"

"Connor, sir."

"Don't 'sir' me, boy! I'm a park keeper, not a

judge," he said, retrieving first the tin and then the prized yeti scalp.

"I can see you'd want this tin back. Lovely old thing this is, but shall I throw these bits of coconut away? Eh? What was yer name again?"

"Connor. *No! Sir!* No … err. Sorry. No, please don't. I'll take it home. It's precious. It's … It's … It's all part of a … of a science experiment we're doing in the holidays. The others wanted to ruin it for me because, erm, they haven't done their homework. But thanks to you, it'll be alright now."

Connor began to make his way clumsily towards the man. He might be as good as his word, or maybe he was trying to fool him, just waiting for the police to arrive.

"My name's Trevor. Me and Jezzer had a bet you'd be back. We see it all in this park, I can tell yer."

He extended a helping hand. Connor stood there, smelling like a giant wheelie bin, still not quite understanding how events had turned out like this.

"You're in a state, boy. We would have stopped you earlier, but you snuck in without us seeing. Like James Bond you are. Bit messier than 'im though. But now we can see how important this little thingammy is to you."

"It's a … It's a science experiment, at school,

you see, as part of our exams. *Really* important. Err … we have to see what difference occurs to the coconut in the open air, y'know, and the coconut in a closed tin, being in … in the same air all the time. D'you see? In the tin. We can't open it, the tin, not even for a second, 'til err … until we get back to school."

He was beginning to believe himself a little. This was pretty convincing stuff. Should he grab it and run? Trevor was about the only person locally he was confident he could out-sprint.

Connor was appalled at his bedraggled image in the tiny mirror over the hut's wash basin. James Bond? Not just at the moment. He scrubbed as much grime away as possible and straightened his clothes and hair. The small television screen hadn't been showing BBC One at all. Instead, it had four images of various parts of the park on its flickering screen.

"I was no good at school, no good at all," Trevor peppered the air with his thoughts. "I hated it. Some idiot said that yer school days are the happiest of yer life. Huh! What a load of rubbish." Trevor chuckled. "Rubbish – y'get it?"

Connor joined in with a generous smile at the bad joke. Trevor pushed a mug of tea in Connor's direction across a small table. He sipped at the brew gratefully, after ladling in three sugars, plus one more for luck.

"Yeah. Yer like me, boy," Trevor continued. "Large. I've always been large. Tall–large I mean, and I've always been fat–large as well. And I ain't never been able to do a damn thing about it. I've always had this," he said, indulgently patting his large stomach. "My 'bay window', my wife calls it – more like a conservatory now though, she said this morning."

Connor nodded and smiled, but was thinking more about how he could escape. He decided conversation would be a good tactic.

"I get into trouble sometimes, when I'm with my mate Freddie. He was here with me today."

"Yeah. I know the boy. Small lad with mousey hair."

"Hmm. Well the other kids, they always pick on us."

"Yeah! We saw you get attacked. When me and Jezzer went round there, we heard them go on about something you had in yer bag. The scrawny kid was saying that you had some secret thingammy. They were looking for some hidden tin. Nasty lads, that lot. My pride and joy, that patch is. There's signs up saying: 'Don't go near the shrubs.' They won us park of the year 1997, those beauties. Anyway, whatever they were after, it wasn't in the bag they'd nicked off you. So, me and Jezzer put two and two together. I told you, we're not stupid. We emptied the bins once they'd gone and had a quick sort out. Jezzer put the bag from your bin up the front of the cart and he picked out your carrier bag, easy as anything, first time lucky. Always bin' lucky has young Jezzer. Eh? Ha! Ha!" Trevor laughed heartily again at another poor joke. "Bin! Bin lucky! Get it?"

Connor smiled again, as generously as he could.

"We knew it was important coz your mousey pal came round here trying to act all natural. Ha! Ha! But he legged it before I could give him his stuff back. I called after him, but he must have thought he was in trouble." Trevor paused. "I'm not frightening, am I?"

Connor shook his head, trying to convince *himself* as well as Trevor.

"Will you tell yer mate I'm sorry I scared him? I was a bit worried to be honest. I came and sat in here for a minute or two. I hate seeing wrong uns get away with things. So anyway, I kept yer tin, and yer coconut all nice and safe. I knew you'd be back."

"Thank you, Trevor. Thank you very much."

Trevor slid the bag across the table towards Connor's shaking hands. He looked inside it. Tin? Yes! Two pieces of yeti scalp? Yes! Ah! *Three pieces of yeti scalp*. The monastery's treasures were multiplying. One of the cones had split in two. This was not good. Freddie would go mad.

"Sorry about your coconut," continued Trevor. "Jezzer sat on that by mistake. Good job we didn't throw it away though. He was going to. You still be able to do your exam with the three bits, eh?"

"Oh! Yes," Connor gushed, nodding. "Probably make it easier."

This whole tale was getting stranger and stranger; the latest twist being the destruction of an ancient Nepalese relic by a junior park keeper. Not even the head park keeper, but his lanky young assistant. How would they explain that back in Nepal?

Connor was tired and drained, but most of all, he was hungry. The mug of tea only reminded him that his stomach needed filling. *Chips*. That was the answer. He daydreamed about pouring salt and vinegar over them, whilst Trevor chattered on.

"We never put coconuts in tins in my day. Don't even remember having coconuts then. I wouldn't go back to school for nothing."

Then, more seriously, leaning forward he continued, "You listen to me, Connor. I still see the people who bullied me at school. They drive around in their BMWs and their four-by-fours and they all got angry faces. They're still shouting, to this day! I see the boys who gave me hell, shouting on their mobile phones. They're men now, with families, and I see them being angry with their wives, and their kids, y'understand? And then I see the kids being angry with other kids, over *nothing*, silly things. It's all a mess, Connor, d'ya understand? If a silly old park keeper with a big bay window like me can see it's wrong, why can't they, with their degrees and their company cars and …?" he trailed off.

Trevor was a pretty amazing bloke really. Then, with a smile returning to his huge face, he said, "Don't be one of the angry ones, boy. Promise me that? If there's one thing I know I'm right about, it's that. Just don't be one of the angry ones. We've got enough of those already. Anyway, be sure to let us know yer results."

"What results?"

Trevor shook his head, tutting. "Yer coconut results – how you get on."

"Oh! Of course. We'll come and tell you, Trevor. Thank you very much. I can't really explain how important these are, all I can say is – thank you."

"Get along now, it's late. Go straight home. *Ask* next time. All right? Tell your mousey pal an' all. We won't bite."

Connor walked away, carrying the precious cargo. He had to sit on the bench by the bus stop for a minute to reassure himself of his achievement and allow it to sink in. He pulled a James Bond face and pointed his finger like a gun. Cool.

He could go the quick way home, down the dark back streets and risk tripping and shattering the yeti scalp beyond repair, or he could go the slightly longer way home, via the well lit high street and the chip shop.

No contest.

Chapter Eighteen

After half a mile Connor began to relax a bit. He attracted some strange looks as he passed The Fox and Pheasant, but no one challenged him. There were still a few people about and he had to queue at the chippy, to the amusement of some and disgust of others.

"What's that 'orrible smell? It's rank," shrieked a loud, blonde girl. She moved aside and Connor was soon served and on his way, avoiding any eye contact.

He stood in McKenzie's shop doorway with the valuables of Thyangboche secured tightly between his feet. He savoured each and every glorious chip. (He'd ordered a sausage in batter as well, but that hadn't touched the sides.)

He was approaching that terrible moment when you see the vinegary, salty bottom of the bag and you realise there's only a few chips left. *I could always go back and get another bag*, he thought when … BANG.

The punch landed remarkably close to the bruises from the day before. Connor dropped the remains of his supper. The chip bag split and shed its precious remnants onto the pavement. Another swipe grazed his arm and deflected to his right, striking the newsagent's metal shutter.

"Aargh!" shouted Jasper, pulling back his hand. He'd caught his bare knuckles on the serrated metal of the security screen. Jasper stepped back holding his bleeding fist. Connor just stood there, alone and terrified. Again.

Through his brimming tears he saw there were three of them this time. Jasper was bent double, but he would soon recover. His hardest sidekick, Maz, aimed for Connor's chin, but hit him on the shoulder as he turned to avoid the punch. Maz lost his balance as he swung with his other fist, slipping on the spilled chips. He landed heavily on that bone at the bottom of your back, yelling in a burst of agony.

Although Connor had been hit and winded, he was beginning to feel a little invincible. His two main opponents were already down.

That left number three – it was Kelvin. He looked frightened. He knew he wasn't going to get the better of Connor, being half his size. Connor stood his ground, the bag at his feet, ready to defend it to the end.

Jasper was beginning to straighten up and Kelvin was egging him on.

"I heard them. I did, Jasp. Him and that Freddie. There *was* som'ink in his rucksack, honest. But they must have hidden it. He finks he's been to China or somewhere, somewhere freezing. Been up mountains, he says. He's a nutter, that Freddie. I heard 'em. They were in the oak tree, all afternoon. I was lis'nin. They nicked a tin off a bloke called Mindy. They hold hands an' all. He was being chased by a gang of monks or somefing – and this tin's got treasure and everyfing."

Kelvin's monologue had given Jasper time to recover. His shadow loomed over Connor once again.

"Been where? Where's Freddie been? China?" cackled Jasper, trying to laugh his pain away. Then his scary blue eyes locked onto Connor's and his mouth contorted into the familiar sneer.

"Been where, Fat Boy? Oh yeah, Kel, he's soft alright, that Freddie, but not as soft as someone else I know, eh, Connor? Not as soft as you, you great fat penguin. Been holding hands with Freddie, 'ave you? You been to China 'n' all, 'ave you? No chips in China, Connor. Do penguins eat chips? Eh? Fat

Boy! Do they?"

As his fist came flying forwards, Connor ducked at the last second. Jasper's good hand crashed against the sharp metal edges of the grill. The impact was far harder this time and immediately there was far more blood. As Connor looked around at the others, Maz slapped him on the top of his head and the shock of it sent him crumpling down on top of the carrier bag.

Connor was not going to let them get it. He huddled into a ball with his hands around his head and the bag well protected beneath him. Every ounce of his being was set to defend it.

"Help me! Someone! *Aarrgghh!* Help me! *Pleeaasse!*"

Kelvin felt brave now and launched a kick, which succeeded only in catching the top of the concrete step in front of Connor's head.

Connor heard the snap of bone as Kelvin's toe broke under the thin leather of his trainers. He lay on the pavement, rolling in agony amongst the squashed potato. The smell of the vinegar on the pavement made Connor feel sick. Maz pulled his head upwards and Connor promptly vomited all over him. As Maz tried to scramble away, he fell over Kelvin and banged his head hard on the pavement.

So, it was just Jasper to worry about now. Connor

still didn't fancy his chances. As he bent down to grab the bag, Jasper swung his leg viciously. The impact would have taken Connor's head off if he'd connected. Sadly for Jasper, he slipped in a mixture of chips and sick. In what looked like a classic cartoon moment, he travelled up in the air and down hard onto Kelvin, who was doing his best to stand back up. Now all three lay in a heap on the pavement, covered in blood and regurgitated chips.

Connor would like to have taken total credit for this victory, but he had felt strangely protected. It was like he had a force field around him.

The small crowd that had gathered to watch the entertainment drifted away. No one had been brave enough to help.

With the bag clutched to his chest, Connor hugged the shopfronts for a hundred or so metres until he heard the sirens. Then he ran and ran and ran, all the way home.

The relics of Thyangboche had been bruised and battered like their protector, but at least they were safe.

That had been Saturday. It was Wednesday now. It took three days for Connor to recover. He felt really bad on Sunday, worse on Monday, and only started smiling a bit on Tuesday when his mum brought him up a doughnut. She'd actually been quite concerned. She knew Connor didn't put these things on. There would be no point. Sympathy didn't exactly fly around their house at the best of times. Connor was surprised when her head poked round the bedroom door, pointing to a piece in the local paper about street violence, drink and drugs. When she asked him if he was involved, he just repeated what he'd said on Saturday as he crept in, covered in his and other people's blood, vinegar, chewing gum and sick. He said he'd been started on by some lads who wanted his chips and that he didn't know who they were. He told her he'd spent the day with Freddie in the woods, and had never thought of a life of crime, or juvenile delinquency. He told her drink and drugs were not on his agenda and that he was more interested in writing essays and keeping score for the cricket team. She watched the doughnut vanish, then reminded him how inconvenient it was that he was at home all day, needing her constant attention. That was more like it. Connor recognised his mum again. She was back to normal.

His parents had actually been pretty good on Saturday. They calmed him down and got him washed. They had to throw all his clothes away. His mum cursed the expense of buying new stuff, but his dad got out his beard trimmer and sheared Connor's hair off, using the longest setting. It was just easier to start again.

So now he had hair two centimetres long all over, except for a few straggly long bits at the back which his dad missed. *I'll have a go at them myself sometime*, he thought, whilst surveying his new look in the bathroom mirror.

Despite being battered and bruised, Connor was thrilled that he had held out. It was by far the bravest thing he had ever done.

He really hoped that Jasper, Maz and Kelvin's injuries would last until school started. It might lead to a bit of respect, or at least a truce.

Freddie rang on Sunday evening. He asked the questions because he could talk openly and Connor gave short, awkward answers because he was in the lounge with his parents. He thought if he left the room they'd be suspicious.

"How are you?"

"Not so good."

"Why?"

"Got attacked by some kids, after my chips."

"You alright?"

"Yeah."

"How about the … y'know?"

"Fine."

"You sure?"

"Yeah."

"How many of them?"

"Three."

"What, Jasper and Paul?"

"No."

"Well – Jasper?"

"Yes."

"Maz?"

"Yes."

"Who else?"

His mum was trying to listen.

"Not that Kelvin?"

"Yeah."

Connor tried to give Freddie the whole story like this, and at last his mum's nose pointed back towards the telly. Connor managed to convince Freddie everything was safe.

"Well done, Connor. *Really* well done.

"How's your sister?"

"She's had a baby boy. They've called it Finlay."

"Oh brilliant. Tell her congratulations."

Freddie rang again on Monday. Connor filled him in on all the missing details. He hoped he hadn't over-exaggerated. Connor could count five separate purple shapes and wanted the bruises to last until Freddie got back from Cornwall, so he could see how brave he'd been.

He had promised not to look in the tin and had been true to his word, but he looked at the scalp quite a lot. He'd tried to see if it could be mended. The section that was broken looked like it could easily be glued back together, but he thought he might wait to see what Freddie said.

He made a list of things to take to Nepal and raided his coin jar to supplement the meagre curry and rice diet. It may have been right up Freddie's street, but Connor knew he would need some crisps and nougat to see him through to the next dal bhat.

While his mum was out shopping he packed his warmest clothes and as much food as he could find. How would ginger nut biscuits cope with the vortex? There was only one way to find out.

Freddie rang at three o'clock to say he and his dad were back. Connor scribbled a note saying he was staying over and left it propped against the microwave where he knew it would be found.

Mr M was unloading the car when he got there.

"You look like you've come to stay for a week!" he joked.

"Seeing as your mother's still fretting over that pink screaming thing down in Port Isaac, we'll have a proper boy's night, shall we, lads?" Mr M suggested.

Connor knew he was really chuffed about his grandson, and 'pink screaming thing' was said with a crafty smile and a knowing wink.

"Now vanish. Go on, now. I'll grab you both

later and we'll get a curry supper."

Connor closed the bedroom door, ready to show off his wounds, but Freddie interrupted, "Connor, there's something else."

"What?"

"It's not just Mallory's tin and the yeti's scalp." He paused. "Look at this."

Freddie produced a green and red patchwork doll, bursting at its seams. He handled it like a policeman with vital evidence.

"What is it?"

"I found it in Callow's bag."

"It's a doll!"

"Yeah! Of course it's a doll. But look … Look inside. Go on."

Connor took the doll and turned it over in his hands. The back seam had split, revealing some once white stuffing. But that was not all. A tight roll of green banknotes completely filled the inside. He pulled out the roll of notes and held them, as if weighing up the possible amount. It was heavy and smelt like really old money does; used by a million people.

"How much? I mean, whose is it?"

"It's either Callow's or Svensson's."

"Well. How much is here?"

"It's dollars. It's American dollars. Look, you can see the …"

"How much Freddie? How many dollars?"

"Well about, fifteen."

"Fifteen? What, fifteen hundred?"

"Er, no. Thousand."

"Thousand? Fifteen thousand dollars?"

"Yeah! About that, yeah!"

Chapter Nineteen

"Fifteen thousand!"

"Yes. U.S. dollars. Fifteen thou—" Freddie's voice trailed off. Seeing his friend's reaction reinforced his original shock.

"Let's get this straight. You found fifteen thousand dollars, stuffed in a doll, in one of the bags, with the yeti's scalp and Mallory's tin?"

"Yes. That's right. And it's fifteen thousand, six hundred and forty-two," Freddie added, as if he'd been withholding vital information.

"Fifteen thousand, six hundred and forty-two dollars," Connor repeated, as if it would help clarify matters.

After the leap into the chasm and the return home, Freddie had examined the bags.

Scalp safe – good. Tin safe – brilliant. The other

contents were three cigars, a lighter and a ferocious looking pocket knife, plus return air tickets and two passports, one English and one Swedish, belonging to Michael Arthur Callow and Uri Stig Svensson. Freddie was thrilled they would be left without the stolen treasure, passports, money and return tickets to Chicago. Why Chicago?

"But the doll? The dollars, I mean," Connor asked, still baffled.

"They were there all the time in the doll. I just thought it was a present for his daughter or someone, so I put it in my bag ready to go to Cornwall, to give to the baby. Then on the drive down, I tried to clean it up a bit … that's when I discovered the money." Freddie had been amazed and had counted and recounted the cash until his hands stank of it. *Dirty money*, he thought. *Dirty money – for dirty work.* He was convinced it was the payment for stealing the treasures. It was a large enough amount of money now, but in 1989 it would have been an even bigger fortune.

What should he do with it? It would be a useful sum to the Malones, who weren't exactly rich. But how would he explain it?

Typical, he thought to himself. *The one time in your life you stumble across a fortune, and you can't do anything with it.*

The obvious answer wormed its way to the front of Freddie's brain. It took a while to get there, but eventually it arrived: *Take it back to Nepal, if I can get back. Take it back to Thyangboche, to help rebuild the monastery.* He had been thinking of buying his parents a holiday, or paying off some of their mortgage, but the only real answer was obvious.

Connor and Freddie stared at the money for a bit, then sprung into action and sorted out their kit for the journey.

"First – clothes," said Freddie. "No need to pack too many. Wear them all. It'll help cushion the knocks in the tunnel. Second – food …"

"Right," said Connor, assuming total charge. "I've bought a few things …"

Freddie burst out laughing as the duvet was suddenly submerged under bags of sweets, fizzy drinks and crisps.

Freddie edited the pile, keeping the more high-energy foods to help deal with fatigue in the mountains. Connor looked longingly at the rejected items and hid some fruit chews in his left pocket. Freddie grabbed something from his desk.

"Oh, I nearly forgot! I bought this disposable camera. You keep hold of it, Connor. You can be official expedition photographer. You're much better at all that type of stuff." Connor put the bright yellow camera in his right trouser pocket.

Freddie got a flask from downstairs, then he wanted to see the injuries. He gasped out loud as Connor bared his battered torso. It still looked very dramatic. He was shocked. "Thanks, Connor," he said. "You really are the bravest lad I know. No one else would, y'know, do what you have. Thanks."

"That's all right," came the proud and honest reply.

Connor told him about Trevor the park keeper. "We ought to thank him properly, once all this is over," he said to Freddie.

He tried to explain about 'Young Jezzer' sitting on the yeti's scalp, but kept sniggering with nervous laughter at the thought.

"I think we should leave the scalp as it is," replied Freddie.

"We could pin a note to it, explaining what happened."

Freddie smiled but then went silent for a moment.

"I went to the library in Padstow. I found out as much as I could about Thyangboche and Namche Bazaar and stuff. Look." He moved closer so they both could see. "I wrote some things down: 'The ancient parchments are beyond value. They were written by Padma the Wise, just like Mindhu told me, and another book said: 'They are lucky to still be in existence.' Listen to this: 'Having mysteriously survived the terrible fire in 1989, the sacred teachings of Padma the Wise are said to contain all the knowledge and wisdom the world will need if humanity ever has to start again after the 'War to end all Wars'."

"How about that, Connor? 'Padma hid the twenty one most valuable relics of Tibet, in twenty one secret valleys in the Himalayas.' Just think, Connor, I was dragging the secrets of the world's future through the flames. I don't think I would have managed it if I'd known how important they were."

Freddie talked about Mindhu and proudly produced the hair wound in a tight circle, tied with a piece of red cotton and hung from a string around his neck. He let his friend hold the momento. Connor was just thinking how things were going so well. The evening felt perfect; hanging out with Freddie, getting prepared, feeling excited and more than a little scared about what they were about to do. Then …

Disaster.

Connor returned the lock of hair, being extra careful so as to not damage it, holding his breath until the handover was complete. He placed the keepsake in Freddie's palm, then shot his arm back with a huge flourish, exaggerating the success of having returned the precious item. As he did so, he swept Mallory's tin off the bed with his elbow. It launched through the air in a fatal arc. Connor and Freddie watched it turn, end over end, heading towards the wall. Connor knew it would hit the wall and burst open. He just knew.

Both boys made attempts to catch it. Connor got as far as raising his left arm and stretching out. Freddie leapt off the bed and made a despairing dive. It thundered into the wooden skirting board. The ancient leather strap that had held the tin so tightly shut for so many years gave way and the lid popped off the priceless container.

Freddie thudded into the bottom of his chest of drawers a split second later. The room went completely silent. As Connor began to open his mouth to apologise, Mr M called up from downstairs.

"You alright, boys? Hey, Freddie, if you're wrestling Connor, there's only one winner there, boy. Submit now, whilst you've still got some teeth."

"No ... I just tripped, Dad," Freddie yelled back.

The last thing they needed was Mr M coming in and asking questions about what they were planning to do, with the room covered in all their kit. They looked at each other and held their breath, desperately hoping not to hear footsteps on the stairs.

"I'm so sorry," Connor started, but Freddie held up his hand.

"Let's see what the damage is first," he said calmly. Freddie knew it wasn't intentional, but if there was film of Mallory and Irvine's successful ascent of Everest and Connor had exposed that film to light, it would be completely ruined. Connor felt exactly like the gross waddling penguin that Jasper had so expertly performed.

Freddie gently moved the contents, one at a time, to see if there was any film.

"What do rolls of film from 1924 look like?"

He used a pencil to sort through the things, gently pushing objects to one side.

No film.

They breathed a huge sigh of relief. Connor felt sick, but incredibly thankful. He sat back and let Freddie do the investigating. There were old Victorian photos of a very upright family, staring stiffly at the camera and one beautiful oval-shaped photo of a very pretty woman. Freddie offered it to Connor, but he just looked from a distance, feeling he had done enough damage for one day. Freddie turned to the letters. There was a message of good luck from The Royal Geographic Society in London, and one from his wife, signed 'Your ever-loving Ruth'.

Next came a set of handwritten notes on how to operate the oxygen cylinders by a man called George Ingle Finch. He ended: 'Take it surely and steadily, old man. Although not with you this time to hold your hand, we all walk with you, every scrap of the way. Your loyal friend, Finch.'

It was a totally spine-tingling experience for Freddie, to know they were looking at the great man's possessions, having learned so much about him at school. There were lots of scrawled sketches and some poems on cards. Suddenly Freddie sat bolt upright and his mouth fell open. In his hand he held a very well-thumbed copy of 'If—' by Rudyard Kipling. Wonder sparked in his eyes as he realised he and Mallory were driven by the same magical words. Separated by generations, but united by a beautiful poem.

"You'd better learn it, Connor. I'm sure that's what opened up the vortex. Practise it, so you can get back from Nepal ... if anything should happen to me."

Connor scribbled it down as quickly as he could and tucked the note into his left pocket with the chews.

It was all wonderful memorabilia, but it seemed the tin wasn't providing any answers, not for them, Mallory's family, or the waiting historians.

They returned everything to the tin and puzzled

over how to secure the broken strap. Connor's suggestion to glue the strap to the lid in one or two places with superglue won the ideas competition. Freddie acted like he'd completely forgotten that Connor had caused the disaster in the first place. Connor was so relieved that no harm had been done, but he shivered again at his stupidity and how he could well have denied History its answers.

Freddie went for the glue and returned with a water bottle as well.

"We have to drink lots of water at altitude, Connor. This will be for when we first get there."

It fitted neatly into one of the side pockets of Freddie's rucksack and once the yeti's scalp (which was now cradled in bubble wrap) and the mended tin (not looking bad considering its ordeal) went in, his bag was nearly full.

Excitement was mounting and Connor was hungry. He casually disposed of two cans of drink and some crisps that hadn't made the selection process and watched Freddie tuck a couple of extra things into his bag, including his old trainers. Why would he need them? He was already wearing his fantastic boots. Connor didn't ask. Freddie always had a good reason for everything he did.

Finally, with all the kit packed and stowed in the wardrobe, they went downstairs to order the curry. Uncle Patrick had arrived and was sitting on the sofa. He cradled a glass of his favourite Irish black beer and stared adoringly at the 'pink screaming thing' in a series of photos on his laptop.

"Well, Freddie, me boy! How's it feel to be an uncle?" said *his* uncle. "If Finlay's half the boy you are, the world will be a richer place. This little bundle is the latest magical thing to happen to our family. We're the luckiest people alive. I hear both you boys have been in the wars since Sunday. Been fighting off the girls have you, lads?"

It was a perfectly nice evening, but neither Freddie nor Connor could really concentrate. They were both too wound up about the impending possibility of time travel. The food was fantastic and Connor managed to finish everyone's leftovers, so he had a good 'full tank' to begin the adventure. He also drank lots of water to prepare for the high altitude. He didn't want to let Freddie down and he was determined not to make any more mistakes.

Mr M and Uncle Patrick treated them to a few stories about their wild youth in Ireland, and Freddie's favourite uncle finished by saying, "Ah! You boys wouldn't believe the adventures we got up to. We were quite the explorers. We got about. But there was never a scrape we couldn't get out of. I hope you two have as good a time as we did. Adventure after adventure – those were the days, eh! Declan?"

As they said goodnight and retreated upstairs, past the smiling faces in the photos, Connor hoped and prayed that by the time he walked back down the stairs, he would have travelled to the roof of the world and back.

They didn't know for certain that Freddie's vortex would open at midnight, or even tomorrow, or next week, or ever.

"It just feels right, Connor. Trust me. It's going to happen."

In the hour and half they waited, Freddie checked and rechecked everything, whilst Connor showed his nerves by eating all the unwanted provisions.

Midnight approached and they positioned themselves ready, holding all their kit on their laps. They moved the foot of the bed into the room slightly, so it pointed directly at the map. Then they sat side by side waiting for the vortex to open.

Connor laughed nervously, Freddie checked his watch, and they both tried to concentrate on the map. Minutes seemed to take an eternity to tick by. They could just about hear midnight strike on the church clock in the distance and both boys braced themselves for lift off.

Nothing.

One minute passed. More nervous, expectant giggles from Connor.

Still nothing.

Waiting was hard, it really was.

Nothing. Still.

Connor was now holding his breath, making him feel a little light-headed. Freddie told him to relax and started mumbling, "Namaste," very quietly. Connor copied him, but soon burst out laughing again.

It was 12:03 a.m. now. Connor suddenly felt the need to go to the toilet. He'd been fine standing up, but sitting perched on the end of the bed was placing far too much pressure on his bladder.

Nothing. Five minutes had passed since the midnight chime.

Freddie was the picture of concentration, totally focussed on the map. He was reciting 'If—' now, over and over in a whisper. Connor was hunched, pouring with sweat and biting the handle of his daysack. His bladder was bursting.

It was no good. He would have to go.

12:10 a.m. *Nothing.*

Connor was about to explode. He dropped his bag and ran from the room, telling Freddie to wait for him and only just made it to the toilet on the next landing.

He was trying to be as quick as possible. "Come on! Hur–ry up!"

He charged headlong back into the bedroom and closed the door. As Connor turned into the room, he was dazzled by an amazing sight.

Coloured lights, words, numbers and what looked like electrical charges darted and swirled around the tiny space. It had been completely calm and quiet outside on the landing, but inside the room the noise was deafening. Shouts. Music. Laughter. Horses. Engines. Every sound imaginable enveloped Connor as he stood, rooted to the spot.

He held up his arm in front of his eyes to shield the glare from the strobing images and staggered towards the end of the bed where he'd been sitting next to his best friend.

Freddie was gone. "Oh! No!" He was gone.

Desperately, Connor looked up to the map on the wall, the wind forcing his eyelids wide open. There was Freddie, looking like someone desperately trying to hold some lift doors open. He was fighting hard to stop the map from closing. He had one arm and leg in the bedroom and his head and the rest of his body in the swirling tunnel beyond. He beckoned to Connor, but as he did, the wall shrank even further and he had to force his shoulder back into the gap to try and keep it open. Connor struggled against the torrent, trying to make it to the wall.

"You can do it!" Freddie shouted.

He could see how hard his companion was trying. The hole was getting smaller all the time.

Freddie's body was crumpling in an effort to keep it open. Connor summoned up all his strength and grabbed Freddie's left hand. He stuck his left leg and arm through where Freddie had been, then he bent double and tried to squeeze his body into the tiny gap. He was just too big for the opening. It was impossible. Freddie pulled and Connor struggled. The wall began to feel sharp and painful around his shoulder as the hole continued to close.

Freddie pulled himself fully into the tunnel to give Connor more room, but it was no good. It was absolutely no good. The vortex was trying to whisk him away and he had to hang on with all his strength.

"You go!" Connor shouted to him. "Go on. Go … Be careful. Bring me back a prayer scarf." He had *so* wanted one for himself.

Connor was distraught. He hated himself again. He hated himself so much. He couldn't believe he had missed the greatest opportunity of his life because of his weak bladder. His anger raged into the tunnel and his frustrated cries mixed with the maelstrom beyond. He had no option but to retreat. He tried to pull his tortured body back into Freddie's bedroom, but he was stuck. His left arm and left leg were being battered around in the vortex while his head, body and right hand side were back in the third bedroom of an ordinary suburban semi-detached.

The map closed around Connor's shoulder and hip. He was now completely set into the wall; stranded and helpless, with his aching arm disappearing into Russia and his leg floundering somewhere in the Indian Ocean. It was as if he had become part of the house. "I know I wanted to live with the Malones, but this is ridiculous," he mumbled, through brimming tears. He was stuck fast, completely trapped by the brick and plaster.

"The chance of a lifetime and I've blown it. I've blown it big time."

So that was it. Connor couldn't tell the time, as his watch was on his left hand inside the tunnel, along with the chews and the poem in his left pocket. He could feel the wind swirling about his arm and leg on the other side of the wall, and yet in the bedroom all was quiet. Maybe he should wake Mr M and Uncle Patrick, but how could he possibly explain the complete disappearance of their precious Freddie, not to mention his superb impression of a breeze block. Calling them would have to be the last resort.

He was angry at everything now. He tried to remember bits of Kipling's first verse, but gave up in a shower of self pity.

"Can things get any worse than this?" he wailed. *Yes they could.* The thought of what was in his pockets made him realise that he still had the camera. Freddie would not get his picture of Mindhu. Connor felt as bad now as when Mallory's tin had burst open.

He would just have to dangle out of the wall like an inflated cuckoo clock.

But hold on.

Freddie would be back from his adventure tonight, even if he was in Nepal for days, wouldn't he? That's what had happened the first time.

Freddie certainly wouldn't have any trouble finding his bedroom, what with his big oaf of a best friend's arm and leg flailing around in the vortex.

As the time passed, Connor tried to calculate how long he'd been there. He was convinced that it was at least four or five o'clock in the morning, but then the clock on the church struck one. Time doesn't exactly fly when you're hanging out of a wall. As he mulled over all the options and the variations on all the options, he slowly drifted off.

Connor woke to three soft chimes from the church bells. Not long afterwards, he felt the wind increase on the other side of the wall and a minute or so later, two hands grabbed his arm. Convinced it was Callow trying to rob his watch, Connor struck out blindly. His arm was forced roughly against the wall and gradually the pressure started to release around his shoulder. He felt the plaster begin to liquefy. Then the map opened and when the hole was big enough, it welcomed a battered training shoe into the room and Connor was suddenly free enough to flop down onto the floor. Freddie landed on top of him a split second later. The wall closed and the map sealed, as the sounds from a thousand disappearing portals faded away.

They sat up and looked at each other with expectant grins.

"Guess where I've been," whispered Freddie.

"On the Bakerloo line to Namche Bazaar?" Connor offered.

"Yeah! How did you guess?"

"Fruit chew?"

"Thanks, I will."

Chapter Twenty

Dishevelled, clearly shattered and with that same haunted look in his eyes he'd had when he'd returned the first time, Freddie Malone sat next to Connor on the floor of his bedroom. The wall was closed and the map perfectly intact. It was impossible to believe that just thirty seconds ago one of them had been part of it.

From deep within his layers of clothing, Freddie produced a pure white prayer scarf. "For you, mate ... I wanted to get you a stick of rock with Thyangboche Monastery written through it, but they don't sell it anywhere." He held his hands up to halt the flow of questions and simply said, "What's happened here? Tell me everything. What's the day? The time? Just while I get my breath. I'll tell you everything, but you go first. Please."

Connor brought Freddie up to date with the

news from the bedroom, which didn't take long. Freddie was relieved they were still in the early hours of the same day he had departed. He was very taken with Connor's descriptions of what it's like to be a wall and laughed, especially when Connor said he'd thought Callow was stealing his watch. So despite trying to let him rest, Connor was finished in no time and waiting patiently for the final jigsaw pieces to be revealed.

"OK. OK," Freddie sighed. "Where do I begin? Is it really only three hours since I went? I can't believe it. Anyway ..."

He closed his eyes, sighed and began, as Connor finished the chews.

Freddie had tried frantically to pull Connor through the closing hole, but he could see the wall was becoming solid. "At least your head was the bedroom side, so I presumed you could breathe. All these frantic voices in the vortex were rushing me to the Namche portal. I was shot along the tunnel much faster than the time before, as if the vortex was trying to make up for my delay. I bounced off the walls, trying to protect the rucksack."

The voices were talking in loads of languages, pleading with Freddie to hurry up.

Eventually everything shuddered to a halt and he

found himself in between a view of Namche Bazaar and the scary desert portal he had seen before. Freddie looked at the endless, rolling sand dunes and saw the same poor man crawling across the sun-baked desert. The legionnaire staggered to his feet, screaming his wretchedness, then stumbled and collapsed.

Freddie tore his attention away from the legionnaire and hauled himself over to the edge of the Namche portal. He could see immediately that it was changing. The far left end of the vista had become grainy; grey and static. There, it had already set solid. As Freddie's eyes scanned across the portal, the colour and movement returned. Where he stood, it was as alive and vibrant as ever. He knew that time was short, that the portal was closing forever. "Hurry," a chorus of overlapping voices said. "Your chance will soon be gone! The portal is dying."

At the rate the greyness was spreading, Freddie reckoned he had about thirty seconds. The date codes spun furiously. Just as he was about to climb through, a crystal clear death cry cut through the chaos of the tunnel, quite impossible to ignore.

Freddie stepped back and saw the outstretched arm of the dying man in the desert, pleading desperately for help. Freddie reached for his water bottle and tried to push it towards him, but the wall bent and warped and would not give. He scrabbled in his trousers for his house keys, picked the longest and sharpest and rammed it into the plasma barrier. It split instantly and Freddie thrust the bottle through into the man's grateful grasp. As Freddie pulled back, the man begin to drink. Then, like a camera panning away and up high at the end of a film, what lay beyond the dune was revealed. There was a large walled town, easily within crawling distance. Freddie knew that the man would survive.

He was now in real in danger of not getting through the rapidly greying Namche portal to return the treasure, which was, after all, the real purpose of his journey. The date clock was counting in the bottom right hand corner at a ferocious pace. As he watched, it moved from April 1995 to January 2001. There was now no hope of getting back to Namche for 1989, unless he waited for the clock to go round again. How long would that take?

Freddie plunged at the wall and hurled himself through. By the time he landed on the other side, many more years had passed by on the speeding clock.

Freddie looked back to where he could see its fading reverse image. The numbers had stopped turning and were set. He concentrated hard to work out the date backwards and was heartbroken to realise it was April 2019.

"2019! No! Please! You've got to take me back to 1989. Pllleeeaaassse!"

His desperate cry echoed around the mighty hills

and mountains.

Nothing was left of the portal now except a faint outline, like an empty picture frame and even that quickly disappeared. Freddie was back on the familiar hillock, overlooking the wonderful vista that had first transfixed him, not just a week ago, as it was in real time, but now over thirty years ago.

He was devastated that it was not the same date as before. What could he do? Should he recite 'If—', go home and try again? Deep down, he knew it was hopeless. The portal had closed forever from the vortex side and his dream of Mindhu must end.

If he hadn't stopped to give the man water, he would have got back here in 1989, or at worst 1990. He could have returned the treasures and lived a life of adventure with Mindhu.

Only two problems with that, though. One: every time he closed his eyes to try to sleep he would have seen the dying man's outstretched arms and heard his screams. Two: he had left his best mate set solid in his bedroom wall. Whilst *he* would have a wonderful life, he could not consign anyone to an existence as a wall hanging, certainly not Connor – probably not even Jasper either.

Heartbroken, Freddie set off downhill towards Namche. He could go straight to Thyangboche to sort everything out, or he could catch up with life in Namche first and personally deliver a special present he'd brought with him. Really and truthfully, he wanted to catch a glimpse of Mindhu, who now had to be in her forties. Just one glimpse before returning the treasures. One last look.

He was soon pacing along the level section of path by the sanctuary of Lally's hut. Instead of the tiny shack he had expected to see, it had now doubled in size and had a lovely vegetable garden, with goats and chickens roaming in a side paddock.

Freddie stopped and leaned against the wall. A flood of happy memories invaded his mind, a week ago for him, but thirty years for Lally, Mingma, Saylor, Elvis and Ghito. What would have happened to them all?

A very old man appeared around the corner, feeling his way cautiously and carrying a large walking stick in his other hand. It appeared to Freddie that he was now blind. He was very wrinkled and bent-over, but unmistakably Lally. He sang a reedy tune as he picked his way to a wooden seat, perfectly situated in the brilliant morning sunshine.

Lally hovered over the bench like a helicopter does before landing, with his hands checking underneath him to see if it was safe to sit. He flumped down, the way old people do, and made himself comfortable. He peeled an apple expertly with a pocket knife, threw the skin to his chickens and imitated their thankful clucks.

Freddie couldn't walk past and not say hello. After all, Lally was obviously blind, and nearly two generations had passed. *He won't remember,* Freddie thought as he walked tentatively towards the old man who was now serenading his chickens. Long before Freddie got anywhere near Lally, he fell silent.

"Namaste," he said genially. His voice was much higher pitched and scratchy.

"Namaste," replied Freddie. "May I sit, and talk, sir?" he added respectfully.

"English–man ... yes sir, with old Lally. Sit ... comfort please." Freddie usually corrected people who called him English, but he quite rightly let Lally off and took his place in the sun, gratefully accepting an apple. He exchanged pleasantries with the old sirdar until he was brave enough to talk of times past.

"I was here, a long time ago, over thirty years, maybe longer. I met you then, you were very kind to me, and also to a friend of mine."

"Ah! Good. It is always my ten'tion ... my *in–*tention, to be kind."

"Well you were, Lally, very kind. How are Saylor and Elvis?"

"You know those boys?" Lally chuckled. "Ha! Ha! Those boys. They big rich yak men now. They got yaks," he chuckled. "Big, rich, men, very funny. They good to me, bring me chang when yaks go past."

"They bring you chang. That's good."

"They big rich boys now. They build Lally new house, after earthquake, very 'spensive. Many, many rupees. They treat old Lally ... like King of Nepal. They rich boys with big stack of rupees. Big as a mountain. Ha!"

Lally was clearly pleased that someone knew of his exploits from way back.

"Ah! You remember Mingma? Good sherpa boy. Mingma now very busy. He now sirdar like me, not good as me though, Mr English," he cackled and showed Freddie how few teeth were left in his mouth.

"Mingma unlucky man. All fambly missin' after lan–slide in Langtang Valley. Four years now missin'. Aftershock as big as first earthquake. Very sad. He still trying to climbing Sagarmatha. He still try ... Always the weather drive him down mountain. One day maybe?"

"Ghito, the cook?" asked Freddie

"Old now, old cook ... old like his food." Again he laughed and slapped his hand on his thigh, cackling as he wiped tears away with his scarf.

"He fat old cook, cannot walk ... not like me. I is still strong."

Freddie was desperate to ask about Mindhu, but was scared of the answer he would almost certainly get.

"So Saylor doesn't have to dig the toilets any more?" Freddie smiled.

"No, big rich yak man Saylor. He has many people dig his toilets ... no more digging toilets, Mr English.

You know Elvis? You see him? Not since long time. Ha! Ha! Ha!" Lally now dissolved in fits. "Well Elvis ... He bald now! True. He *bald* Elvis! Very funny. Everyone still call him Elvis though. He bald man now ... Ha!" Freddie laughed with Lally.

There was a brief silence. Lally lifted a hand and touched Freddie's face, examining the contours and features. He concentrated and seemed to drift away. He eventually shook his head, letting out a little laugh that became a sigh.

"You 'mind me of someone, long ago. But he dead boy now, gone. We all sad when this boy, also English. He fall off cliff. In Namche. Yes. He was our friend. Our Mr Freddie!"

"Freddie, yes, he was my friend too," Freddie said. "He told me all about you, and Elvis, Saylor and err ... and Mindhu." There. He had said it.

"Mindhu yes, Mindhu." Lally was in a reverie. "We all sad ... good strong boy, die over cliff. Why? Why he do that?"

"We don't know, Lally. That's why I've come back, I suppose, to find out."

He had said it once so he had to say it again, "And Mindhu?"

"Mindhu. Yes and Passang. Passang brother gave yaks to Elvis, for prezz–ant. But Passang – an' Mindhu too, is famous brother, sister ... sherpa, sherpana ... We all proud of them, very proud. You not know 'bout them?"

"No, I'm afraid not, Lally, no."

"Ah! Passang climb Sagarmatha, your Everest. He climb nineteen. Ah yes … ninety-four. Nineteen ninety-four. Yes, but bad fall on way down, and no … no longer good to climbing."

"But he's alive and well?"

"He's alive, and very bad legs and back, but alive … alive yes!"

"And Mindhu?"

"Yes … and Mindhu sherpana. Very famous. Has climbing your Everest three times, our Sagarmatha. How you call it? Two thousand and one year, she climb first time. Then long gap, very busy … and now also twice in last few years. Three times she climbing. Very good. Very famous."

Freddie's heart pounded. He had a vision of the beautiful, smiling girl scaling the peak and a flood of affection overtook him. He sat in the bright morning sun with tears rolling down his cheek, pecked at as they hit the dried earth by the circling chickens. Mindhu had climbed to the highest point on Earth three times.

What a girl, he thought, then corrected himself. *What a woman.*

"Is she back in Namche, at her home?" Freddie enquired bravely, now no longer feeling like a stalker.

"No … she giving talks to climbers. At Thyangboche. She climb again Sagar— Ah! Your Everest. She climbing

… this year again. She talk in Thyangboche I think. She can talk very good. She talk … back legs off a yak. Haha!" he cackled again, thinking this his funniest joke so far.

After a pause, Lally spoke passionately about surviving the terrible earthquake and resulting avalanche in 2015, when twenty-two climbers and sherpas died at Everest Base Camp. A small fraction of the 9,000 people who perished across Nepal that day. He followed with happier tales from even further back in time, about the years of hard work rebuilding the monastery following the fire in 1989. The whole population had helped and vital funds had been raised by Sir Edmund Hillary, who had toured the world raising money, not only for Thyangboche but also building new schools, a hospital and a new airstrip at Luckla.

The monastery took five years to complete and the magnificent statue of an even bigger, happier, smiling Buddha was proudly unveiled. Although there was still great sorrow that some of the famous treasures were gone, the immense joy of the new building largely overcame the pain of the disaster.

"We, man – woman. We have always to live on … Fire, and even bad earthquake – the hurt, the dying, cannot stop the world smiling. We must smile if something is funny … cannot stop our spirit, our will, from surviving. This is how Mindhu climbs Sagarmatha.

She has the will to go on ... to survive. To live life for all those ...err. All those who not got chance she got. She spesh–shul."

He faded, and after a few moments when he seemed to have nodded off, he jerked and apologised to Freddie, saying, "I go lie down now. Sleepy Lally!"

Before shuffling around the side of the most beautiful retirement cottage in the world, he turned to Freddie, raising his scarf higher around his neck, as if to ward off a chill.

"Aah! A man. A very fri'ning ... fright–*ing*–ning man. Yes you understand? A very fright–ing–ning man. He still search for Mr Freddie. In the valley. He looks, days and night. He search in dirt and rocks. Yes! For Mr Freddie. He says Freddie has something ... that belong to him. But he is mad, wild mad man, like a yeti. Yes! Dane–juice. He looks wild like a yeti! Maybe he get all Elvis hair now. Ha! Ha! He steal Elvis hair and put it to his head ... Ha! Ha!" He stopped his laugh and said simply, "We ... We miss Mr Freddie. It is good we remember him, Mr English." Lally raised his arm, as if tracing Freddie's features again, like an artist at an easel.

"You 'mind me of him ... you Mr English. You 'mind me of this boy. He is the boy who Mindhu climbs for ... because ... he never had the chance. Yes, her Mr Freddie she calls him. It's true. She will climb again for Mr Freddie. To take his spirit to the top of the

234

world! To let it blow free. In the wind. To fly high above us, forever. He is here with us now ... Yes ... I can feel him."

As a light gust of warm breeze ruffled his straggly hair, Lally turned away. In his high reedy voice, he started singing, "Resham fee–ree–ree, Resham fee–ree–ree ..."

Freddie sat still on the bench in a trance as the sound faded. As the long lost boy cried for what might have been, the chickens and goats nuzzled his legs as if to try and cheer him up.

Chapter Twenty-One

There was only one direction Freddie could take, and it led him, step by breathless step, ever closer to the beautiful, lonely and sacred monastery of Thyangboche. The difficulty of the journey was lost on him and only occasionally did he stop to eat or drink. Lally's words echoed in his mind, confusing his thoughts and emotions. Callow was alive and still looking for the treasure, and Mindhu had dedicated her three ascents of Sagarmatha to him.

Somewhere behind him was Callow, and somewhere ahead of him was Mindhu. He doubted now whether he had the strength left to carry out his mission. Maybe he should leave the treasures here for someone to find.

No! If Mindhu climbed for him, if she risked her life over and over again in an effort to release his spirit, the very least he could do was fulfill his small part of the bargain. He would find the strength from somewhere.

Each step took him nearer to her and further from the hateful Callow.

By late afternoon, as he climbed the last few hundred feet to the plateau, he felt strong again. He crested the final ridge and he caught his breath as he saw the new Thyangboche for the first time. A magnificent building stood before him, with white walls and red roofs, sheltering scores of windows and balconies. From the ashes of the terrible fire, Freddie saw that a new, brave and more beautiful phoenix had arisen.

The compound was packed with monks and tourists, tents, climbers and trekkers. Little shops and houses had spread out around the edge. Next to the monastery was a new visitor centre. Freddie made his way cautiously through the doors, guarding his precious cargo with mounting excitement.

In one room was a display of photographs, showing the rebuilding work following both the fire and the earthquake. In another was a small shop selling postcards, books and prayer scarves. Freddie bought one with the remaining rupees from his previous visit. He crossed to a small hall where a hundred or so chairs were set out. There was a small, raised stage in front of a white wall, which had a square of light projected on it, no doubt ready to show photographs or a film.

Freddie's heart stopped.

Before him was a poster with the details of a lecture to be given that evening. More importantly, on the poster there was a photograph. A picture of a smiling, confident climber, clad in high altitude survival gear on the top of a mountain. She was dressed in blue and grey, except for one tiny splash of colour. It was a picture of Mindhu standing on top of Everest, with a red handkerchief tied around her neck.

People headed towards the monastery as the deep horns sounded. It was time for the afternoon ceremony.

Freddie caught sight of a collection box. The sign read: 'For the continued restoration of our beloved monastery and earthquake relief.' He carefully produced the tight roll of 15,642 dollars. No one saw him push the notes in clumps through the top of the box. As he crammed in the last two single dollar bills, a monk rounded the corner and told him that prayers would begin soon. Thanking him for the donation, the monk scuttled away.

Freddie smiled and made his way into the new temple.

It was bigger and more magnificent than before, with brightly coloured wall panels surrounding a sea of maroon-clad monks at its centre, still drinking tea to stave off the cold, still chanting in little rocking motions, still breaking off occasionally to stare at unusually dressed trekkers.

Overseeing it all was a grey-haired, bullish looking old man in thick glasses, whose face was unmistakably that of the High Lama. Behind him, rising a good five feet taller than the original, was the happiest smiling statue you could ever wish to see. His arms had been carved resting in his great lap, with the fingers interlaced and the palms upwards, no longer having the need to point to any clues. To the left stood a cabinet not dissimilar to the original, with two empty shelves.

As the prayers finished and the monks filtered away, Freddie slipped around the back of the Buddha. When all was silent and dark, he retrieved his torch.

In pride of place were the teachings of Padma the Wise, the secrets needed to rebuild the world, if we ever destroyed the present one. Freddie could not help thinking that the wrong relics had been stolen. However important Mallory's tin and the yeti scalp were, what could be more important than the answers to existence?

This was the most critical moment, but getting into the cabinet proved impossible. They had obviously tightened security since 1989. Freddie could only open it by smashing the glass. He shone the torch around, seeking inspiration, and the bright beam caught the sparkling eyes of the smiling Buddha.

"Of course! That's it! That's perfect," he whispered. He moved cautiously over to the statue. In the Buddha's right palm he laid the three sections of the yeti scalp, and in its left he placed the tin box containing Mallory's precious possessions.

Freddie stood looking at the humble offerings to the great Buddha and he caught the face of the statue in his torch beam. It seemed to Freddie, that the Buddha had an even bigger smile on his face now.

During the service, he had again watched the tea boys come in and out of a small door on the far side of the temple. Now, in a matter of seconds, he was into the courtyard, through the gates and over the wall, his duties almost complete. He had donated the money and returned the lost relics. But he was not going to go without at least sneaking a final glimpse at the yak train driver, who had stolen his heart and carried it with her to the top of the world.

Freddie was nervous and excited. He waited in the freezing shadows until he heard a polite round of applause signal the beginning of the talk. His plan was to sneak in at the back and make himself as invisible as possible. He could see under the door that the lights had gone out and the projector show had begun. He entered in the darkness between two photos. When the searing white beam shone again, he was already sitting like a church mouse right at the back, clutching his bag.

His heart leapt as into the beam of light stepped Mindhu. Not the Mindhu he had left only a week ago, but a lean, toned, strong and radiant woman. There was still the recognisable smile and her voice was little changed, except her English was even better. It was as if he was looking at the future. In one sense, of course he was, but how different would that future have been had his best friend not been stuck in a wall and he not stopped to give the dying legionnaire water? He watched the graceful figure illustrate various slides and he comforted himself that he could not have sat there happily, knowing he had ignored the outstretched arms of the dying man. It was extremely painful nevertheless.

"This slide shows the sherpas burning iuniper branches at base camp. It is called a *puja* ceremony, wishing for a safe expedition and a speedy return. These blocks of glacial ice in the Khumbhu Icefall can weigh a thousand tons, and can topple over at any moment. It is one of the most unpredictable parts of the mountain. I have known many people die here. My own brother, Binoi, did, many years ago."

People around Freddie asked questions and, peering into the darkness, Mindhu answered knowledgeably and humbly. Freddie sat transfixed in his seat.

The slides scaled the mountain, taking the audience with them. After the Icefall came the sanctuary of the Western Cym. "This has best been described as a 'Cathedral of Silence'. It is a magical and tranquil place." Then on to the Lhotse Face, a huge six-thousand-foot ice wall. "Which really sorts the men out from the boys." Mindhu's cheeky grin sparkled as she said it.

The room was warmer now from the radiated heat of the projector. Mindhu stopped for a drink of water and took off her outer fleece jacket. There, as proud as anything, around her neck was the red handkerchief, caught in the beam, shining out like a beacon. Freddie's hand went to the coil of hair, and for a moment they were joined again, as they had been over thirty years before.

A South African climber, two rows in front asked, "I notice in all the photos you have that red scarf, can you tell us about it please?"

"I will, yes of course, I will. When we get to the summit, I will tell you, sir."

More pictures, from the danger of the Lhotse Face, out, up and over the Geneva Spur, to the relative tranquillity of the South Col – tranquil only in the respect that it was relatively flat and you could pitch camp – here lay the remains of dozens of previous expeditions. Their ruined tents, empty oxygen bottles and the long dead bodies of climbers who would never return. It was as much as people could do to get themselves down off the mountain, without carrying the body of a colleague as well. They lie perfectly preserved in the permafrost.

"You must remember, this is the 'Death Zone'. Above twenty-six thousand feet, your body literally dies. No cells replenish, no illnesses get better."

Then she described the gathering of strength for the final push to the summit, away from the South Col, constantly talking to the Goddess and asking her permission to continue. Long, hard, dangerous hours followed, up to the famous Hillary Step. Once this was negotiated, the way was open to the top and the lung-bursting, head-splitting, limb-tearing effort to place one heavy boot in front of the other to reach the ultimate destination on earth.

Then the moment the audience had waited for, the joyful series of pictures of Mindhu and her climbing companions clustered at the roof of the world, smiling, praying and celebrating. Mindhu had made each and every person in the room feel that they had climbed with her. She had taken them all to the top of Everest.

"Bingo," she said, which seemed to be a very strange word to describe the moment, but Freddie knew exactly what she meant.

Following the group photos, there were two of Mindhu alone. The first was the familiar shot of her, with gloved hands joined in prayer underneath her smiling face, with her goggles pushed up high on her brow. Then a close-up, with the Himalayas slightly blurred behind her, sadness pouring from her huge brown eyes and with her right hand touching the red handkerchief at her neck. There was a short silence as Mindhu looked at the picture, mimicking the photo in real life.

For the first time in over an hour her voice wavered and she seemed unsure of herself. Without looking at the audience, but fixing her eyes on her image, she said,

"This reminds me of someone very special. Someone who would have given everything to be able to stand where I have – on top of the world. He has gone to the place where all lost climbers go – to the biggest and most beautiful mountain in the sky. The only way I have to be with him, is to take this scarf with me. So his soul can fly on the wind. His spirit is still there … still at the top. In some ways he is lucky. I have to climb up and down, but he will always be there … Always. He can look at the world and see who is good, and who is bad. He can see what is wrong and what is right. He helps me reach the top … He talks to me … He is with me every step of the way. As he would have been, in life … Had he lived."

"Who was he?" asked the South African, after Mindhu had fallen silent.

"A boy. Just a boy! A boy I once knew a long time ago, who died very young. I climb for him, and also my lost brother, Binoi. I take their spirits for walks to the top of Everest … and I share the view of the world with them. My lost boys."

No one stirred. Freddie sat and stared ahead, his vision blurred by tears that brimmed over, then cascaded down his cheeks, finally lost in his fleece.

Two more photos followed. Mindhu being presented to Government officials and receiving an award, and then a family group. Next to her was a slightly older man with a huge grin on his face and an arm around

244

her waist, and most notably, a completely bald head. Thirty years on, Elvis looked very kind and funny, and obviously cared for and loved Mindhu very much. "This is my husband. My other rock!" she said. Two small girls completed the family group and already Freddie could see the resemblance to their beautiful mother. Their smiles were carbon copies of the girl he had seen that first morning. He noticed one other thing. Both girls wore beautifully knitted pink cardigans, almost identical to one seen a very long time ago on a child in Namche Bazaar, who had nearly been lost under the thundering hooves of stampeding yaks.

The hall's few dim lights were turned on as Mindhu concluded. Freddie pretended he was tying his boot laces, so as to remain invisible.

"I offer only three thoughts, which you can think about, as you walk and climb." She spoke again with the original conviction in her voice.

"Take only photographs – and leave only footprints." The phrase hung in the air, to be followed by, "It's the journey that's important, not the destination."

Again, there was a silence whilst her eager audience took in its meaning.

"And please ... take someone with you on your adventures, someone who is not so lucky. Take their spirit with you, to enjoy the view of the world. That way you will never be lonely."

A rousing standing ovation greeted her final bow,

and as Freddie made his way unseen from the room, Mindhu signed autographs at the desk. He ducked around the other side of the door by the collection box and caught one last lingering glimpse of the beautiful woman. He would always remember her, but not like this. He would think of her as the girl he had first met, when he was the boy he once was.

Time to move on, he thought.

He was just leaving the Visitors' Centre, when an excited young monk pushed past him, shouting and waving his arms and hands. The others in the shop leapt to his side as he jabbered and pointed wildly at the monastery, explaining something in frantic detail. Then he turned to the trekkers and said, "The treasures! Our lost treasures! The relics of Thyangboche are returned! The lord Buddha has found them. Our monastery is whole again."

The monks hugged each other. Then horns blew, cymbals, gongs, drums and shouts echoed around the frosty plateau. People rushed towards the temple. A wave of euphoria swept through Thyangboche. Excited groups spoke in dozens of languages, translating the news.

Freddie stayed well out of the way, observing from the shadows and smiling to himself. Although it was a freezing cold night, he was warmed by the effect his actions had on these wonderful people.

Everyone rushed to the temple, including Mindhu,

who passed not ten feet away from him. The happy shouts and cries continued, piercing the thin night air. Freddie watched with a smile, but after a while he retreated and created a nest in the straw of one of the yak herders' huts on the rim of the plateau. He knew he would be safe here, as he had seen its previous resident drink a whole jar of chang to himself and that man was now snoring happily in an adjoining hut. People danced, sang, drank and rejoiced long into the night.

As he drifted off to sleep, his mind saw a hand touch a piece of red cloth, and a peace overtook him. It was like no other feeling he had ever experienced. It was a calm that envelopes you when you know you have done something properly. A calm only matched in a pair of shining brown eyes. Eyes that had viewed the world from its highest point. Eyes in which a part of him would be lost forever.

Chapter Twenty-Two

It was well before dawn when Freddie awoke, frozen to the bone. He left Thyangboche for the last time, a broad smile on his face. He decided not to wait for the money to be discovered. He was happy to imagine what would happen. Instead he turned to his final task and trod the path to Namche Bazaar like a seasoned local.

The news had spread fast. After all, there were internet cafes and satellite phones in the region now, and so a stream of people was heading for Thyangboche. Freddie revelled in the excitement and pleasure he had created. Entire families were on the move, several generations picking their way excitedly to their spiritual home.

He strode past the hillock and smiled as his return portal shimmered briefly, promising him a safe return in a few hours' time. Expectant ghostly figures crowded the translucent opening, calling his name, eager to whisk him home. With his confidence restored, Freddie concentrated on the steep descent.

Eventually he entered a deserted Namche and made directly for a particular house. The passing of time had changed remarkably little in this part of the world.

A hundred yards short of Mindhu's house, Freddie slipped off his rucksack. He pulled out his battered training shoes, took off his walking boots and wiped them clean. Inside the left boot he placed a present that he'd bought in Padstow, and inside the right he placed a rolled up folder. Then he tied the laces together and attached a label, which read: 'For Mindhu.' He placed them by the front door, knocked loudly, retreated up the street and peered back from the safety of a low wall.

After a few seconds, Elvis opened the door and looked out. As he made to move back inside, he noticed the boots. He bent down suspiciously and picked them up. Again he looked left and right, then turned and closed the door behind him.

Sooner or later, Mindhu would return to Namche and Elvis would say, "These were left for you." She would take the boots and even if she didn't recognise them at first, when she looked at their contents, she would understand. For inside the left boot was a roll of pink wool, the sort you would make a cardigan with for a little girl. Inside the right was a rolled up school folder, containing a project. 'Everest 1953–2018 by Freddie Malone.' Then she would realise that she no longer had to be sad about Freddie – that he was still alive. She could take someone else on her climbs. After all, he had been to the summit three times already and was about to go on a fourth expedition to the top of the world. It was someone else's turn.

It was time that Mindhu let go of Freddie – and time that Freddie let go of Mindhu. Never to forget each other. But to let go. Simply that. He knew the boots might confuse Mindhu and maybe even upset her, but in time she would be happy that he was alive and must have had good reason to do what he had done. He knew she would link the money and the returned treasures with his offering at her front door.

He walked away, head down, deep in thought. Had he done the right thing? He thought so, and in the end, that was all that mattered.

Freddie made his way to the market square. He stood alone in the deserted clearing, as pleased with himself as he could ever remember being in his life. Things didn't normally work out so well. He ambled towards the stupa. Beyond, he could see the edge of the huge cliff where he had slipped and fallen on his last visit.

Then a huge hairy hand grabbed him by the throat and spun him round, lifting him clean off his feet. In one terrifying split second, the world had turned on its head. And far from being all right, it was now all very wrong. Really, very badly wrong.

Callow's eyes danced in a devilish smile as he clung on to his long lost enemy.

"I've been looking for you, boy," he growled. White spittle flew into Freddie's face as he spoke.

Freddie's throat was burning. He could hardly breathe.

"I've been searching for something. I hear it's made a magical reappearance. Everyone's gone to see it ... It must have been *you*!"

Callow dumped Freddie on the ground, grabbed his right arm and twisted it up behind his back, making him scream in pain. Callow may have been an old man now, but he was still as strong as an ox.

"I've been searching that river bed for thirty years, boy ... up and down that valley, searching for just *one* sign – *one* clue. I've been looking in the wrong place, haven't I? Where you been hiding, boy? Tell me! Tell me!" He hoisted Freddie close to his foul-smelling body. Callow seemed to have completely forgotten to wash for three whole decades, and his breath was even worse.

"Tell – Me – Boy! – Tell me! What trick did you pull on me? Eh? I saw you, boy ... I saw you plunge off that cliff."

Freddie desperately searched for help, but the town

was empty and he couldn't shout out because Callow's other hand was clamped tightly over his mouth.

"I've been here thirty years, looking for what's mine – thirty years, boy! Why haven't you grown up? Who are you, Peter Pan?"

At this he laughed like a madman. Thirty years of scouring the valley bottom, unable to work out how boy, relics and money had completely vanished, had driven him to the edge of reason. He was now a slavering, haunted beast of a man, who made the Callow of old seem like a puppy dog.

"I've got some questions for you, boy, and before you die you're going to answer them."

Callow dragged Freddie towards the cliff edge.

"Poor old Svensson. He'd like to be here now to see you, but he's dead. Yes – dead. And soon, so will you be! We had to go home empty-handed – to explain to someone, why we didn't have certain *things* ... certain things we'd been sent to get, for a certain *collection*. Someone was very upset with us for not bringing those *certain* things back. Are you listening? It's because of you boy, that he's dead. It's your fault. I want to know boy, how you survived that fall?"

He dragged Freddie to the edge. Callow removed a tattered belt from his greasy trousers. He tied Freddie's hands together behind his back, looped the belt around a metal post, knotted it tightly and stood back to survey his prisoner.

Freddie shouted, "Help! Pleeeaase! Somebody!"

Still no one came and Freddie knew that this time he was done for.

Callow pulled a rusty metal tube out of his jacket which he unscrewed to reveal a half-smoked cigar. He looked at it longingly and smelt the shabby object, as if it were a rose.

"I've been saving this," he said gravely. "I've been saving this, Peter Pan. My last cigar. I've been saving this for when the end comes, or for when I got certain articles back ... or for when I found your bones."

He lit the filthy cigar and along with grey blue smoke there erupted the unforgettable smell, now slightly preferable to the stench of Callow himself. His eyes revealed bloodshot, broken veins amidst the haunted glare. Callow fixed Freddie with his terrifying gaze,

"You will tell me everything. E–ver–ry. Lit–tle. Thing. Boy! While I smoke my cigar. So I understand. And then you will die. *Talk*, boy."

Just then a gaggle of porters climbed the final steep yards of the path into the far corner of the square and Freddie, seizing his moment, cried again for help.

"Help! Help! Please! Please Hellmmpff!"

Callow pounced to smother his cries. The porters stared, dumbfounded at the incredible sight; the huge, monstrous man grappling with a boy who was tied to a metal pole. They moved slowly towards the evil giant as he rocked Freddie back and forth. This loosened

253

the belt around his wrists a little, but also did the same to the post. Its crumbling footings began to spew over the cliff edge. The porters dropped their huge loads and scurried to help Freddie, who was dwarfed in the huge man's grasp.

As the porters arrived, the post finally split the fragile cliff edge away. Man and boy, locked together, spilled over and into the chasm. Callow let out a terrible, shuddering, desperate cry.

They spun and twisted in the air, falling like a lump of granite into the abyss, as Callow continued to hold onto Freddie with a vice-like grip.

Freddie moved his arms down his back to get them under his feet. Callow grabbed his wrists, but the giant's fingers moved the belt slightly and one of Freddie's hands came free. He was able to bring the pole round and began to hit Callow however he could. Blow after blow landed, but seemed to have no effect.

In a flash of inspiration, Freddie spread one arm out and immediately started them spinning more violently. At the same time, he started shouting, tucking his chin into his shoulder to avoid the rushing air and get the words out.

"If – you – can –"

Each word took a breath and a rotation. He punctuated the words with jabs at Callow, using the metal post as lethally as he could.

But Callow clung on.

He screamed at Freddie, "What's this? Witchcraft, boy?" He sounded even more demented than before. "You spouting witchcraft at me, boy? Eh?"

On Freddie went.

Breath. Word. Hit.

"If – you – can – fill – the – unforgiving – minute."

Freddie struggled, but it felt useless. Time was running out. Callow's terrible grip on Freddie showed no signs of relaxing. In a last ditch attempt at anything, Freddie bit down hard into Callow's hand. He bit and bit, ground his teeth and shook his head like a dog.

Callow released his other hand to prise off Freddie's teeth. In a flash of brilliance, Freddie relaxed his bite and was now detached from Callow. He jabbed at the giant's head with the metal pole. Callow grabbed at it desperately as Freddie pushed it hard at him and then let go.

It had worked! They were now separated, spinning downwards at the same rate but in ever widening trajectories. Freddie continued chanting as rock and frothing meltwater rushed up to meet them.

"YOURS – IS – THE – EARTH – AND – EVERY-THING – THAT'S – IN – IT –"

Callow plummeted headlong towards his deserved end, screaming his last ever obscenities, raging at the unfairness of the world.

As calmly as he could, Freddie completed 'If—'.

"AND – WHICH – IS – MORE – YOU'LL – BE – A

– MAN – MY – SON!"

Whereas before he had dived headlong into the water only to find the safety of the vortex, this time he was heading for some huge rocks. He closed his eyes, thought of Mindhu and called to the four winds.

"NAMASTE."

In an instant, Freddie was in the time tunnel. The terrible cries from Callow were cut short as his body thudded into the valley bottom, where he had spent thirty fruitless years cursing and searching.

The turbulent chaos of the tunnel was a welcome relief to Freddie after what he had just experienced. He really hoped that was the last time he would fall off the cliff at Namche Bazaar. Three times would be showing off, surely.

The minute or so it took to get back to the comical sight of Connor's arm and leg sticking out of the wall was otherwise only notable for the desert portal next to Namche, where the words "THANK YOU" were written in large letters in the sand. Then a sand storm obliterated the grateful message and the legionnaire's departing footprints, which led towards the safety of the town.

It had been light for some time. The boys had hardly moved a muscle as the end of the adventure was revealed. Freddie was now silent and exhausted. Connor felt nearly as tired, and all he had done was dangle out of a wall and eat sweets. He had no clever one-liners to make his heroic pal laugh. He felt Freddie's pain and his loss, his joy and his excitement as if he had been through it too. And he was secretly very pleased to have been nowhere near Callow and the terrifying fall from the cliff. It was just as well he had been stuck in the wall, really.

In the morning, Uncle Patrick and Mr M still hadn't stirred. The exhausted boys both had showers, bacon sandwiches and left a note to say they were off out for the day. They made their way to the oak in the wood and slept for a large part of the morning. When awake, Connor didn't refer to Freddie's epic adventure at all. He decided his friend would talk about it if he wanted to. Occasionally, Connor saw him put his hand to his neck and touch the tightly bound hair on the string. Connor found himself putting his hand to the prayer scarf, which was worn proudly round his own neck – and as he did, he thought of Mindhu, Lally and plump smiling Buddhas.

In the afternoon, when the woods got a bit too busy with mountain bikes and screaming kids, Freddie and Connor wandered towards the park. They strode boldly through Jasper country and were treated to the wonderful sight of him and Maz being dropped back home by his mum. Freddie and Connor stood on the opposite pavement as the injured bullies got out of the car, Maz first, with a big bandage wrapped around his head. He turned to help Jasper, but tripped over one of his crutches. They stared angrily across the street, as Freddie spoke in a raised friendly voice, "Sorry to hear about your accident, Jasper. Connor was telling me all about it. Sounds nasty. Hope you'll be alright for school?"

Jasper just grunted, his face in a snarl.

"Connor tells me you found my phone in the park?" Freddie continued.

Jasper's mum glared at him.

"Does that new phone you've got belong to this boy? Well, does it?"

It was funny seeing Jasper scared of his mum.

"I found it! I was looking after it for him. I was gonna give it back when term starts."

"Well, go on then, now's your chance!" she yelled.

Jasper grudgingly handed the phone over, his piercing blue-eyed glare firmly fixed on Freddie. His mum's ear bashing continued as they entered the house.

"Let's not get too cocky," Connor said cautiously, walking on.

Freddie laughed for the first time since his return. It was the relief. But Connor's words rang true. There was no way Jasper would let this episode be forgotten. He would want some kind of revenge. Freddie turned the phone on.

"Hey, look at that. Jasper's got me a twenty pound top up! That's very generous of him."

Connor and Freddie treated themselves to fish and chips and sat in the park, for once feeling completely immune from any danger. Connor offered Trevor a chip, which he politely refused.

"On account of me bay window, boys," he said, contentedly patting his paunch. "I've lost a pound this week. How's that project of yours, with the coconut. Any good? Did yer both pass yer exam?"

"No Trevor, not yet. We're not back at school. But we'll tell you as soon as we do find out. And thanks again for all your help!" said Connor, through a mouthful of vinegary chips.

"No problem." And he was off emptying bins.

Later they saw Kelvin being dragged for a haircut by his mum. He had a big plaster cast on his left foot and didn't see them. The plaster would be on for ages, long after term had started.

They spent the last of their money on ice cream and chatted about everyday, uncomplicated things for a change. At about five o'clock, Freddie said wearily, "I think I might just sleep for the rest of the holidays. I've got to go now, Connor," he sighed. "Gotta go home and think about things for a while

– look up about Mindhu climbing Everest on the internet and stuff. The fire, the earthquake and things. Sort it all out, in my head."

His loyal and faithful companion nodded.

"But I just wanted to say thanks, y'know. Thanks for *everything* – for finding the treasures and ..." He paused. "And for listening." He smiled.

"That's okay. I enjoyed it," Connor beamed back at his best friend.

As Freddie turned to go, Connor thought of something. "Freddie!" he called,. "You know the vortex ..."

Freddie nodded. "Well, have you thought that it all might happen again, y'know – not to Nepal, because that portal's shut. But what about all the others? There were loads, weren't there, like the desert and the guillotine, and the trenches, and ..."

Freddie cut him off with a kind but weary gesture and smiled exhaustedly. "Give me a break Connor," he said kindly. "That's what I've got to think about. Who knows what will happen? I don't know if I'll ever go again. I can tell you one thing, though – you'll be the very first person to find out. See you tomorrow."

Freddie waved and headed home.

Connor stayed on the bench for ages, going over in his mind all that had happened. People came and went, but he was in a different world – a world of proper daydreams. He was surrounded by glaciers and rivers, monasteries and mountains. He remembered everything. The sounds, the smells, the sights and most importantly, the people. He was determined that if Freddie went on another adventure, he would go with him.

Eventually, he came to the conclusion that in order for that to happen he would have to get fitter.

"Bingo! Yeah, that's what I'll do. I'll start tomorrow ..." he promised himself, as he started his second ice cream of the afternoon.

Namaste.

Author's Notes:
The Facts Behind the Story

Thank you for reading Freddie Malone's first adventure. There are more to come! Some of you may be interested to know what's true and what's not in the pages you've just read.

Let's start with **Everest**. As you might expect, the highest point on Earth above sea level is not going to be an easy thing to measure. It's not like standing next to the kitchen wall whilst your mum or dad record your growth at regular intervals with a marker pen.

In 1849, Sir George Everest's survey team measured Peak 15, as it was known then, at about 29,000 ft (8,839 m). Other measurements in subsequent years varied from 29,002 ft to 29,141 ft.

In 1953, when the first proven ascent was made, it was universally held to be 29,028 ft (8,848m).

This is how things stood until an American survey in 1999 anchored a GPS unit into the highest piece of bedrock they could locate which gave a reading of 29,035 ft (8,850m) and with a 'snowhead' height three feet higher than that (although snow/ice thickness at the summit varies constantly as it is in the face of the immense wind speeds of the jet stream).

These are the figures I believe and that I have used in the book. You may disagree. Go and find out!

For the sake of accuracy it has to be recorded that the Chinese and Nepalese have made subsequent attempts at determining the height (in 2005) and they both came up with different figures that they later agreed to compromise on. The figure currently recognised by China and Nepal is 8,848m (29,029 ft). Nepal is planning a new survey soon. Watch this space!

Maybe one of you budding mountaineers will climb Everest one day and calculate its height properly. One thing is for sure, it will be higher when you do so! Due to Earth's tectonic plates pushing together and thrusting the mountain upwards, it is growing by at least a centimetre a year. And do me the honour of taking a copy of this book with you if it inspired you to climb. Take me to the top of the world, please!

Everest has many names. In India it is known as *Deodungha*. It is also recorded as *Chomolungma* (the Tibetan name) on a French map of 1733.

Chomolungma (or Chomulangma) is translated variously as 'Mother Goddess of the Sky', 'Goddess Mother of the World', 'Goddess Mother of Mountains', 'Bird Country of the South' and 'Holy Mother Peak'. All are lovely and all are correct.

The name *Everest* was given by the Royal Geographical Society in 1865 after the Welsh surveyor, Sir George Everest, replacing its previous 'romantic' British survey name of Peak XV.

Sagarmatha is an invented Nepali name for the mountain, originating in the 1960s, and is an amalgam of the Nepalese words for 'sky' and 'head', meaning 'Forehead in the Sky' – somehow less poetic than the Tibetan translations!

1 in 10 is a rough illustration of how dangerous the mountain can be. 2018 should see the 5,000th person to summit the mountain and nearly 300 people have died attempting to do so, not including accidents getting to and from the mountain's base camp. Maths is not my strong point, but thankfully the odds are slightly better than 1 in 10 – but not by much!

Yaks are skittish and unpredictable. Always stand on the mountain side of a passing yak train. Dried yak dung does indeed make an excellent, if pungent, fuel.

Each set of **porters** has a different deal, depending on which trek company employs them. Nepali authorities are trying to regulate their pay, equipment and treatment and things are improving all the time. That's not to say things are perfect, but things are certainly better than they once were.

The **Gurkha** regiments have always been, and continue to be, recruited from hill villages in Nepal and have continually served with British Armed Forces since 1815.

George Mallory died in a fall, high on Everest on 8th June 1924. It was his third trip to the mountain following expeditions in 1921 and 1922. His body lay undiscovered for 75 years until it was found by Conrad Anker on 1st May 1999.

Sadly, there is no known tin of memorabilia belonging to him, although he always climbed with a picture of his wife in his pocket. No picture of Ruth was found on his person, leading many to believe he had indeed climbed the mountain and triumphantly placed her photograph there. As we are unlikely ever to know whether he summited, I have placed the photo of his beloved wife in his "precious" fictional tin.

The oxygen expert from the 1922 expedition, George Ingle Finch, a rather unsung hero, was the father of the actor Peter Finch, but I invented his letter to Mallory.

The famed **yeti scalp** is not at Thyangboche but at Khumjung nearby. Edmund Hillary carried the scalp half way across the world to get scientific verification. But sadly science seemed less than convinced. Judge for yourselves – search on the internet for the 'yeti scalp of Khumjung'.

Padma the Wise is indeed reputed to have written his teachings and instructions for dealing with and avoiding the end of civilisation. But they are not at Thyangboche (sometimes spelled Tengboche).

However, the stone with **Lama Sangwa Dorje**'s footprint (you will be thrilled to know) *is* there and *did* crack in the terrible fire that *did* take place on 19th January 1989. It will not surprise you to learn it was not started deliberately by an Englishman called Callow but by a humble, but equally destructive, electrical fault.

The fire destroyed precious scriptures, statues, murals and wood carvings. Many trekkers helped the monks save as many paintings and books as they could. Edmund Hillary did lead the fundraising for the rebuilding.

There *is* a massive cliff edge and drop away from **Namche Bazaar,** but it is not quite as sheer as I have painted it. Not so very far from the truth though. You would certainly have time to recite 'If—' before reaching the valley floor. It's a long way down.

Finally, take a bow, **Lally, Saylor, Mingma, Ghito, Elvis** and **Mindhu,** who all very definitely do exist – although Mindhu has yet to summit her beloved Sagarmatha. Maybe one day she'll get there.

And maybe one day so will you.

Further Reading

If reading about Everest has aroused your curiosity about the mountain and the beautiful kingdom of Nepal and its wonderful people, I suggest below some further reading for teenagers.*

Into Thin Air, by Jon Krakauer
Facing Up, by Bear Grylls
No Such Thing as Failure, by David Hempleman-
   Adams
View from the Summit, by Sir Edmund Hillary
Also, *Touching the Void*, by Joe Simpson (not about
   Everest, but an essential read nonetheless)

*These books contain descriptions of harrowing events that may not be suitable for younger readers.

Bullying

If, like Connor, you have been the victim of bullying in any shape or form, you will find help, practical advice and most importantly, you will be listened to by people who understand, if you contact:

www.childhelplineinternational.org/child-helplines/child-helpline-network/

www.nationalbullyinghelpline.co.uk

www.youngminds.org.uk/find-help/feelings-and-symptoms/bullying/

www.childline.org.uk/info-advice/bullying-abuse-safety/types-bullying/

www.channel4.com/4viewers/help-support/bullying-harrassment

These websites and helplines provide help, support and guidance for children and parents dealing with bullying, wherever it occurs.

About the Author

Born in Barnet, Clive Mantle has been a well-loved British actor for nearly 40 years. As a boy in the 1960s he sang with St John's College Choir, Cambridge, went to the National Youth Theatre and trained at RADA in the 1970s and has been a fixture on stage and screen ever since.

Clive is best known for playing Little John in *Robin of Sherwood* and Greatjon Umber in *Game of Thrones*, Mike Barratt in *Casualty*, and on stage as Tommy Cooper, and Lennie in six productions of Steinbeck's classic *Of Mice and Men*. His voice is equally well known from nearly 200 audiobooks, and animated characters like Gator in *Thomas the Tank Engine*.

He has been an avid reader ever since being handed *Stig of the Dump* by his parents, and his favourite children's books are the *Noggin the Nog* sagas by the visionary Oliver Postgate.

Clive's passions are walking and fresh air, in the wonderful Wiltshire countryside. Clive's inspiration to write what is now the first in a series of the Freddie Malone adventures came during a trek to the Everest Base Camp for the charity Hope and Homes for Children. He has since returned to the Himalayas and completed the Annapurna circuit.

To find out more about the adventures
of Freddie Malone, please visit:
www.freddiemalone.com
www.clivemantle.com

Thanks

This book would not exist without a great number of people who helped and inspired me along the way.

The two 'Great Kates' – Walsh and Thomas, who got me started and pointed me towards my brilliant agent, Penny Luithlen, who has coaxed, cajoled and championed myself, Freddie and Connor on every step of the journey. Her advice and input has been critical, teaching me to edit eight sentences into five. Then five into three. Thank you.

I am grateful for the encouragement of my friends and family, to all my English teachers down through the years, and for the wonderful time spent reading John Steinbeck and Gabriel Garcia Marquez. I am very proud of, and indebted to, my colleagues from The National Youth Theatre, RADA, and the *Of Mice and Men* and *Robin of Sherwood* companies, who are all lifelong friends.

But mostly I would like to thank my wonderful son, Harry, my parents, Pat and Harold, for their love, support and sacrifice, and my glorious wife, Carla, for her daily inspiration, energy, strength and love.